Because I Need You

Just Because, #1

Drew Duncan

BECAUSE I NEED YOU

Copyright © 2020 Drew Duncan
All rights reserved.

No part of this book may be reproduced or transmitted in any form or by any means, electronic or mechanical, including photocopying, recording, or by any other information storage and retrieval system without the written permission of the author, except in the case of brief quotations embodied in critical articles and reviews. This book is a work of fiction, all names, characters, places, and events are the products of the author's imagination, or are used fictitiously. Any resemblance to actual persons, living or dead, events, or locations is entirely coincidental. All rights reserved. Except as permitted under the UK Copyright, Designs and Patents Act 1988.

EDITING BY: Karen Sanders Editing
FORMATTING BY: Formatting by Leigh

Prologue
Aiden

"The fucking word for this is incompetent!"

I was beyond angry. For the third time that week, the girl had been incapable of following even the most basic of instructions, and it was only Monday afternoon.

Tears welled in her eyes. *Jesus Christ.*

"I'm sorry, Mr Monroe," she sobbed. "I'll get it right next time. It's just that you scare me, and I get all flustered."

Scare her? "Ms Gibbs, you have been a little bit more than flustered, and if you didn't spend as much time on fucking Facebook while at your desk, perhaps you would be able to follow a basic instruction."

The sound of her blowing her snotty nose echoed around my office, and I started to lose the will to live.

"I'm sorry, Mr Monroe." She punctuated every word with a sob.

I didn't understand it. Was there really something so difficult about going down to a different floor, speaking to one specific person, and asking him to provide you with the financial review amendments to the reports from quarters two and three? I mean, I had asked her in English. I'd even said please.

"For the love of Christ, will you stop with the fucking snivelling!" I ran my hands through my hair. I couldn't cope with this any longer. She was just too much. "Ms Gibbs, I think it's best that you gather up your things and go home."

She wiped her nose and smiled. "Thank you, Mr Monroe. I think that would be wise, and I can come back tomorrow ready to give it my all. It's just that my boyfriend dumped me, and I..."

I sighed and cut her off. She wasn't getting it. "No, Ms Gibbs, you misunderstood. *Again.* I don't want you to come back to the office ever again."

A high-pitched yelp erupted from her. "You're firing me?"

Finally, the penny had dropped.

"That's the idea."

The high-pitched noise was back. I lifted my phone. "Douglas. Yes. Right now. My office." I hung up.

Minutes passed, and the noise and the tears and the snot continued. A hard knock on my door signalled Douglas's arrival, and thankfully, this whole fiasco would soon be over. "Come in!" I shouted over the noise.

Douglas, our big, burly security guard, came into the room and took one look at me and then at the woman crying uncontrollably in front of me. He walked over to her, put his arm around her shoulder, and whispered against her ear.

She stopped sniffling, looked at him with red, wet eyes, nodded, and quietly went with him.

Thank. Fuck.

I moved to my drinks cabinet, poured myself a scotch, knocked it back in one, then went back to my desk. I grabbed my phone and dialled an all too familiar number. "Elizabeth... Yes, Aiden Monroe here."

"Am I to assume you need another member of staff, Mr Monroe?"

"Yes, please."

"Can I ask what happened with this one, sir?"

"Incompetence, unapproved internet use, and she stood crying in my office talking about having been recently dumped."

"Ah."

"Indeed. I expect a new assistant first thing in the morning, Elizabeth. And I would like this one to be at least partially decent or I will be forced to take my business to another recruitment agency. Are we clear?"

"We are very clear, Mr Monroe, but I would also suggest that might not be the best solution for you, as we both know I'm the last recruitment consultant in London who is still willing to send you any staff."

"Excuse me?"

"I'll have someone with you in the morning, Mr Monroe."

I didn't say anything further. I simply hung up. As much as I hated to admit it, she was right. I had burned through all the other recruitment agencies in London. In fact, the last time I went looking, several of them turned me down by reputation alone. Elizabeth at Fulton Executive Recruitment was my last chance and my last hope.

Chapter One
Ellis

"I'm telling you, Liz, it's a damn good job I love your face." I laughed when Liz told me who I would be working for.

"I know, I know. He has a reputation." She shook her head.

I groaned. "That's putting it mildly, chick. He's a fucking nightmare. Even I know he's been through more PAs than we both care to think about. I don't know how you deal with that shit."

She shrugged. "He's a well-paying bastard."

"Fine. But I don't want you holding it against me for any other work that comes up after this when he sacks me."

Liz agreed and said she would email me the details; I'd start in the morning at eight. I left the agency office and headed out onto the busy London streets for Victoria Station.

Now, when I said I knew what this guy was like, I didn't actually know him, I merely knew his reputation. From that reputation, I knew he was a tyrant. A lot of the London PAs I knew were in a secret group on Facebook; we talked about the bosses we had, we talked about who was a nightmare to work for, who was hiring... all of it. And one name that regularly came up for being a complete and utter wanker was Aiden Munroe.

I remembered one girl about six months ago who had come into the group to post about him. Her grandmother had died, and she had needed a few days off to help with the funeral arrangements and the funeral itself. He had started with an email and text here and there to ask her about the work he expected her to be doing at home while grieving. Apparently, by the time her grandmother's funeral arrived, he was calling her five or six times an hour and went ape shit when she didn't answer while she had been in church for the service. Poor girl quit the next day. Liz told me off the record that he had called her to see if she would fire the girl anyway because he 'found her level of tardy completely unacceptable in a professional capacity'. Without a doubt, Aiden Munroe was a top-class knob.

Forty-five minutes later, I got off the train in Sutton and started to walk the short distance to the house I shared with my daughter and mother-in-law on Grove Road.

"Honeys, I'm home!" I called out as I opened the door. I heard a little gasp as my daughter ran out of the living room at high speed into my arms.

"Daddy! Daddy! Daddy!" she yelped as she jumped up, and I grabbed her for a big squeeze.

"Hello, monster. Did you have a good day at school today?" I asked my four-year-old, giving her a big kiss on the cheek before carrying her into the living room. "Hey,

Sylvie." I smiled and set my daughter on the sofa beside her nan, kissing the older woman on the cheek too.

"Hello, son. How was your day?"

I rolled my eyes. "New assignment in the morning. I'll tell you about it when the little walls with big ears aren't around."

"Nanna, what's a walrus with big ears?" Addison asked.

Sylvie scooped up her granddaughter and laughed. "I'll tell you all about it later. Let's go make dinner while Daddy gets cleaned up." She winked at me and hustled into the kitchen with my little monster following. I headed upstairs to jump in the shower and wash away the grime of the day.

"Is she asleep?"

Sylvie nodded. "Only took two readings of *The Last NooNoo*."

"Bloody *Marlon the Monster*." I laughed as Sylvie nodded to the kettle.

"Want a cuppa, love?" she offered.

"Yes, please."

"Is that research on the new job?" She nodded in the direction of my laptop, where I sat with it at the breakfast bar.

I grumbled, and she laughed. I read over the pages of information that I could on Munroe Holdings PLC. They owned property—a lot of property—and had since Aiden Munroe's great-great grandfather set up the company in 1912. Jackie Munroe moved to London from Edinburgh in 1898 at the tender age of twenty-three. By the time he was thirty, he owned three properties. Rumour has it, old Jackie was a bit of a gambler, and a good one at that. So good, in fact, that Jackie won those properties in a game of poker. He was shrewd as hell and an amazing reader of people. He spotted their bluffs, poker faces, and tells. The man was a machine. By the time 1919 arrived, Jackie owned sixteen properties and thought that the best way to protect them was to put them into a holding company. By then, he had also attracted the attention of a younger woman called Estelle. He went on to have six children with her and was a millionaire by the age of fifty. After that, the company was passed down the family from father to son, until it had been passed just three years ago from Carter Munroe to Aiden.

I was staring at several photos of Aiden when Sylvie came over and set the mug of tea beside me. Looking over my shoulder, she gasped.

"Bloody hell, Ellis. Who's the hotty?"

I rolled my eyes. "That would be the new boss. Aiden Munroe."

"That the one who wouldn't let the girl go to her mum's funeral?"

I laughed. "Yes, him, but it was her grandmother's funeral, and he let her go, but then harassed her for work while she was off."

"Bit of a knob then, love?" she scoffed. "Good luck with that one. I hope Liz isn't going to hold it against you when you can't work with him anymore."

I pulled her against my hip and kissed her cheek, laughing. "Sylvie, my darling, I would be lost without you. You know that, right?"

"Oh, I know that, son." She couldn't take her eyes off the photos of Aiden. "Shame he's with a woman in all of them. Mustn't bat for your team. I wonder if he likes older women."

I burst out laughing again and slapped her backside, and

she walked off to the living room with her cup. I sat there for a minute, looking at the pics on the screen. Sylvie was right. Aiden Munroe was a beautiful man. But, as she had pointed out, in almost every single image, he had some gorgeous woman hanging off his arm. Working for a man that attractive was going to make for an interesting distraction.

If his behaviour didn't make me want to kill him first.

Chapter Two
Ellis

I was at work by seven-thirty. I wanted to make a good impression on my first day, and I thought that being in thirty minutes early would have been it, but when I arrived, Aiden was already in his office.

"Oh, good. You're finally here." He set an envelope in front of me and walked back into his office. "Read that and do what it says. When you're done, get into my office and we can get started."

His office door slammed shut, and that was the introduction over. No hello, no welcome to the company. I had to be honest; this was pretty much what I had been expecting from Aiden Munroe. The bit I hadn't been expecting was just how much more attractive the man was in real life. I had seen all those photos last night and figured that someone somewhere had been generous with a few filters in Photoshop, but no. He was utter perfection to the eyes in real life too.

I lifted my envelope, opened it, and found a letter inside detailing my duties, a username and password for the computer, what my email address would be, and a few other details I would need, including an online ten-minute test I needed to complete. I logged in, sorted out my email, and got stuck in to the test. Fifteen minutes later, I knocked on Aiden's office door.

"Enter," came the call from inside. I entered the office and paused. "Some ground rules before you begin. I expect you here at seven a.m. every morning. You will be finished for the day by six unless I tell you differently. You will comply with this without complaints about your social life. I expect you to get me coffee, lunch, and anything else I ask you to, including dry cleaning if necessary."

I groaned internally. The man really needed a dogsbody or a wife, not an assistant. "You will type, take shorthand, copy, and anything else I need. You will be responsible for liaising with the heads of departments to ensure that every Friday I have all of their weekly reports. You will manage my diary, arrange my travel, and you will have a company credit card to do all the things I ask you for. Anything purchased on it without my permission will have you dismissed instantly. You are my representation to the whole business. I expect you to be polite, presentable, and amicable. Are we clear?" The man didn't even look up from the report he was making notes on.

Rude.

"Clear as crystal. Anything I can get for you right now, Mr Munroe?"

"There's a coffee place around the corner. I would like a cortado and a salted caramel muffin. There should be a petty cash tin in the top drawer of your desk until you get your corporate card later today."

No eye contact. Nothing.

Dickhead.

"Okay. On my way." I smiled and left his office without

another word, sighing when the door closed behind me. This was not going to be easy at all. The man was living up to his reputation already. I checked my desk for the money he was talking about, found it, and headed back out into the busy London streets.

I returned with his coffee and muffin and left them on his desk for him. He glanced up, and I was greeted with the most beautiful dark eyes I'd ever seen. I froze for a second when we made eye contact, but a brash, *'That will be all, Mr Baxter,'* brought me back to reality, and I nodded and left his office for a second time.

The rest of the day was reasonably uneventful. Aiden stayed mostly in his office, emailing me his demands and calling from time to time to follow up on whether I had completed the tasks that were assigned to me. I had time in HR to file the paperwork they needed for me; various rules, regulations, and a non-disclosure agreement. I was sent to the finance department and collected my company credit card. I had to sign a contract agreeing to repay anything that they ever found to be dishonest use of the card, and that I understood that in such an event it would result in my immediate dismissal. All pretty standard stuff.

When six p.m. rolled around, Aiden emailed me to tell me that was all he needed me for today and that he would see me at seven in the morning. I grabbed my coat and headed home to spend time with my little girl and tell Sylvie all about my new boss and how much of an arsehole he really was.

Chapter Three
Aiden

I walked over to my assistant's desk outside my office door and let my eyes take in everything I saw. "Oh, good. You're finally here." I set an envelope in front of him and headed back into my office. "Read that and do what it says. When you're done, get into my office and we can get started." I closed the door behind me and went to sit at my desk.

Damn. This wasn't what I had been expecting at all.

I had known I was getting a man this time instead of a woman. Part of me hoped that, not only would he be excellent at his job, but that he would also be the kind of man who was nothing to write home about. Well, I got one of those wishes.

According to the agency, Ellis Baxter was amazing at his job. He was fast, he was efficient, he did exactly what he was asked when he was asked; basically he knew what he was doing. I was sure he would be all of those things, but there was just one problem with Ellis.

The man was gorgeous.

And I don't mean in an obvious pretty boy and he knows it kind of way. This was a subtle beauty that came from a man who knew how to carry himself, who was confident of his position in the universe, who had lived and probably lost, and knew how to make it through to the other side of that. Yes, he had beautiful hazel eyes that I could, and probably would, from time to time, get lost in. Yes, he had a handsome face that was perfect in every way. Yes, the boy could dress and dress well. But there was something about him. Something that came with a little maturity and life experience that shone from within.

I'm fucked.

He came back in thirteen minutes later. *Yes, I counted.* I couldn't look up. I focused on the report in front of me, trying hard to look like I was marking up corrections and comments when, in reality, I wasn't taking in a damn thing. I rambled off my usual new PA speech. I had had that many of them in the last year I could probably have repeated it in my sleep.

"Are we clear?" I finished, still not looking up.

"Clear as crystal. Anything I can get for you right now, Mr Munroe?"

His voice was melodic, a rich baritone, and I thought about it saying my name in other circumstances.

I made my demands. Still, I didn't look up at him even once.

"Okay. On my way."

I could hear the smile in his voice, but the very subtle undertone wasn't lost on my ears. He thought I was being rude. He was right. Fucking hell, I was being the most obnoxious cock I could possibly be.

My behaviour didn't get any better. For the rest of the day, I either emailed him or called him. I didn't leave the office when he was at his desk, and I didn't ask him to come in for anything either. Jesus, I really was being a prized prick. I watched the clock for the day to pass, and when six o'clock arrived, I emailed him again and told him he could go home.

Part of me was hoping he didn't come back in the morning, that my behaviour was too much for him. The other part of me hoped and prayed he'd come back and that I hadn't put him off. I wanted to see if he could handle my bullshit. Curious if he was someone I could get involved with. I scoffed at the stupidity of my own thoughts. *As if.*

Chapter Four
Ellis

I WALKED into the building at six forty-five with a coffee in my hand for myself, and a coffee and muffin for Aiden. I was trying to be in earlier than he wanted me to be. I wanted to show that, even if he was going to be a complete arsehole to me, I was going to rise above it and be the consummate professional at my job.

I was ten minutes early when I arrived at my desk. Aiden was already in his office. I settled myself, took off my coat, grabbed my iPad, and knocked on his door. I paused and waited for him to acknowledge me. When he did, I entered with a smile and handed over his coffee and muffin. I lifted the tablet and started to chime off his appointments for the day. When I looked up, he was staring at me.

"Did I get something wrong?"

He coughed. "No. No, carry on." He got up with his coffee and walked over to the window, staring out onto the city street below as I continued.

"You have a meeting with the manager of the thirty-seven houses you have in Dunstable at three p.m. and HR has forwarded his contract and highlighted the paragraphs that pertain to the responsibility he has for the maintenance of the properties and the sections on how any breaches of this are dealt with."

"Thanks for that. There should also be information coming in today from an independent housing inspector for those. Look out for an email from Johnathan Sparrow; he has your email address and mine. I will need the photos he sends over printed out, and I will also need you and someone from HR to sit in on the meeting."

"I'll see to it," I told him, and then carried on with the rest of the diary information on the day ahead. When I was done, I waited for any further input. "Will there be anything else, Mr Munroe?"

"Uh, no, thanks, Mr Baxter. That will be everything."

I thought about it for a second. "Mr Munroe, if it's all the same to you, I would prefer it if you called me by my first name. Ellis is fine by me." I waited for him to acknowledge what I had said.

"Thank you, *Ellis*. That will be all."

I turned and walked out of the office. He was still distant and a bit of a tool, but the sound of my name from his lips sounded so damn good.

That afternoon, Jim Harvey, manager for Dunstable, arrived for his appointment with Aiden. Valerie from HR was already waiting for him, and so was Aiden. The man was late, and he was late on a day when things were not going to go his way anyway. I had printed off the information from the independent house inspector, and I had called him to make sure he was available should he be needed for a conference call.

I knocked on the door to Aiden's office and opened it, putting my head around the frame. "Mr Munroe, Jim Harvey has arrived for you." I could see by his glare that he was not amused by him being late. *Poor Jim.*

"Conference room three, please, Ellis."

Did he just say please?

I nodded and smiled at Jim and Valerie, gathering up all the paperwork I needed as I did. "If you would like to follow me, please. Mr Munroe will be with us shortly." I led the way down the corridor and into the conference room as requested.

Chapter Five
Aiden

I GLANCED OVER ALL the papers I had on my desk. Evidence. Mountains of it. Jim Harvey had been taking the piss on my time, and I wasn't interested in anything that he had to say about it. He was about to find out just how I felt about liars and thieves in my company. A knock on the door interrupted my thoughts.

"Mr Munroe, Jim Harvey has arrived for you."

About fucking time. He was late. It was almost like he was trying to fuck me off even further.

"Conference room three, please, Ellis." I could see the momentary look of shock on Ellis's face at my use of the word 'please'.

I took my time gathering all the paperwork. I didn't need it, but I knew it would waste some time and have the little worm sweating just a little bit longer.

Minutes later, I strode into the room like a king. Unforgiving and unyielding. I didn't even look in Jim's direction. Valerie took out her notepad and started taking notes.

"Mr Harvey, how long is it that you've worked for the company now? Six years, isn't it?"

Jim nodded and agreed, throwing in a 'yes, sir' for good measure.

I nodded at Ellis, and he handed me the first bundle of information I needed; the contract of employment for all of Munroe Holdings' property managers. I picked it up and flicked to the relevant section. "Now, correct me if I'm wrong, Mr Harvey, but we pay you to look after our properties in the Dunstable area, and being paid to look after them means they are maintained to the standard Munroe Holdings expects. Would that be correct?"

Again, I nodded at Ellis, and he handed me the photos that had come through from Johnathan Sparrow. I was impressed. He hadn't faltered or fucked up yet and seemed to know just what I needed when I needed it.

Focus, Aiden.

"Then perhaps you would like to explain these to me?"

Jim wavered.

"These don't look all that well maintained, Mr Harvey. In fact, I would go as far as saying these don't look maintained at all." I outstretched my hand, and again, Ellis handed me exactly what I needed; the statements of Jim Harvey's company credit card. "According to your company credit card, you have been purchasing the items needed for each house as and when needed. I can see a payment here for an American-style fridge freezer. I can also see a payment here for a highly specced laptop. And here, well, this is a payment to the Holiday Inn Express in Dunstable. Am I to believe that we have started to kit out our houses with American fridge freezers, that there was something wrong with your company laptop that you couldn't tell us about, and that we are now putting our tenants up in hotels while we carry out maintenance for them?"

I looked at Jim and watched as the colour drained out of his face. He opened and closed his mouth, but the words betrayed him and wouldn't form.

"Now, I'll tell you how this looks to me, Mr Harvey. It looks like you haven't been doing your job. Not only have you not been doing your job, but you have also been stealing from the company. I bet if we were to pay a visit to your house, we would find an American fridge freezer with this exact serial number standing in your kitchen. I think you know what this means, Mr Harvey."

Suddenly, Jim Harvey found his voice. "B-b-but, Mr Munroe, sir, I can explain... You see... I just... I mean, I..."

I held up my hand in front of his face and he stopped talking. "I thought you might be able to explain, Mr Harvey." I nodded again at Ellis, and he pressed the call button on the conference room's call pod. The house inspector answered, and I introduced the situation to him.

"Hi, John. I was just wondering if you could give me the rundown on the Dunstable properties?" I leaned over the table to let my voice carry to the call pod.

The inspector rattled off everything he had found at the properties. He had spoken to the tenants, and he had inspected each of the houses. Even the very basic problems hadn't been taken care of. One family had been without heating for almost a year. He said it was a simple enough issue to sort out. The house needed a new boiler, and as per the Munroe Holdings' policy, that particular job should have been sorted within fourteen days. He said that approximately ninety percent of the houses were going to need extensive work to have them back up to the Munroe standard. I thanked him for his time, and he disconnected the call.

I turned my attention back to Jim.

Jim looked at the floor. He knew what was coming.

"Right, well, it's very clear to me what has happened here, and it's very clear to me what needs to happen now. Valerie, can you confirm HR's standpoint on this issue?"

Valerie set down her pen, picked up Jim's contract, and read out the relevant section. "*As property manager, the first party agrees to uphold the standards as set out in the Munroe Holdings' handbook. The undersigned agrees that any failure to do so will be treated as gross misconduct and will result in instant dismissal from Munroe Holdings' employ.*"

I nodded. "And about the company credit card, if you please?"

Valerie flicked to another section and continued to read. "*All purchases made on the company credit card must be for the sole purpose of the business. Any purchases found to be for personal benefit or use will be deemed as theft, and as such, will be treated as gross misconduct and will result in instant dismissal from Munroe Holdings. Further to this, the company reserves the right to reclaim the monies fraudulently used and may also report said fraud and theft to the relevant authorities.*" She paused there, set down the contract, and picked up her pen again.

Ellis passed the next piece of information to me, glancing up at me as he did. Just as shit was about to hit the fan, all I could think about was how magnificent Ellis looked. There was something so incredibly sexy about him and how skilled he was in providing what I needed without prompting. My mind wandered, thinking about the other things he might be able to help me with.

"Now, I'm sure you can imagine by my reputation alone what I think might be the outcome here."

Jim blanched.

"You're a fucking liar and a thief. You did it with a flaunting disregard for Munroe Holdings' property and reputation. You treated our properties like a slum landlord would, and you treated our tenants with the same disdain. You stole from Munroe Holdings for your own gain."

Jim gulped.

I tried to keep the anger out of my voice. I wanted to tear this man a new arsehole, but that would do nothing other than temporarily make me feel the tiniest bit better. I hated liars, I hated piss takers, and I hated people who wanted to cause embarrassment to my family's name and business.

A small knock at the door briefly interrupted me, allowing me the time I needed to calm down. I gestured to the police constable on the other side of the glass door for him and his colleague to enter. "Mr Harvey," I continued, "these policemen are here from the Met, and they would like to discuss with you several breaches in building regulations, and the missing four thousand twenty-nine pounds and forty-seven pence from your company credit card. Your employment with Munroe Holdings is terminated immediately, and one of our security team will call to your home address tomorrow to take back your company phone, laptop, and credit card. Or, if you have them with you now, you may surrender them before the police escort you from the building."

He lifted the bag beside him and pulled out his company laptop, phone, and his credit card, setting them on the table.

"Valerie, if you would like to have Mr Harvey sign off on the return of those items and escort him with the police down to the lobby, please?"

Jim Harvey was silent, and the colour had disappeared

from his face when he rose to leave with Valerie and the police officers. I *almost* felt sorry for him. When the door closed behind them, I sighed inwardly in relief.

"Jesus," Ellis murmured, almost too low for me to hear.

I stared. Did he think I had been too harsh? "Problem?"

"No. I'm just astounded that he would treat an employer like that."

I nodded, eased at the fact that Ellis wasn't judging me as being draconian. "It's rare, thank God, but it does happen. Unfortunately, it needed to be dealt with, and in such an extreme case, there is no option for any kind of leniency."

"You wouldn't have contacted the police?" He sounded surprised.

I shook my head. "That is a mess I can do without. If it hadn't been as severe, we usually just let them go and take whatever it was from their last wage or take them to small claims court and sort out a payment plan for it. But that..." I motioned to where Jim had been sitting, "...was a blatant disregard for everything my family built up and stands for."

Ellis nodded, gathering up papers and his tablet, getting ready to leave the conference room. I glanced at my watch. Four-fifteen already. "I don't know about you, Ellis, but after that, I can't be bothered dealing with anything else for the rest of the day. When we get back to the office, call down to Jackie and have her take our calls, and we can knock off early." He looked at me like I had grown an extra head. "You would rather stay here, would you?"

He laughed and shook his head. I stared again. He caught me again. This time, I couldn't look away; he was captivating. His face lit up with his laugh, and again, the sound of him sent a shiver through my body. Damn, I was going to have to work harder to keep myself from chasing him around my desk like something out of a *Carry On* film.

He licked his lips before saying thank you, and I almost came right there in my pants. *Fuck.* I watched him leave before heading back to my office. I was going to be in big, big trouble if I didn't get a grip of myself.

Chapter Six
Ellis

IN THE WEEKS after Aiden decided we could go home early, things had gone from that brief glimmer of good to downright unbearable. He'd been living up to his reputation as best he could. Pure asshole. Yet, every once in a while, I found him looking at me in a way that can only be considered predatory, like I was something he really wanted. Those moments passed as quickly as they arrived, and afterwards, he dialled up the bastard routine to the max.

We had been working hard on buying several big property portfolios from two other holding companies. It meant staying late a lot, and I was starting to feel like the only time I got to spend with Addison was when she was asleep. While I hated being away from her so much when she was so little, I was eternally grateful I had Sylvie to help with raising her. She was in good hands while I worked.

I did have to give Aiden some credit. He'd made sure I'd been paid incredibly for all the extra hours I'd been putting in. When I'd checked my account balance over the past weekend, I thought there had been a mistake somewhere. When I saw it was my wages from the agency, I called Liz to find out what the hell was going on. She told me she had had a call from Aiden, who had told her to double my hourly rate as standard and to give me double time for every hour that wasn't between eight a.m. and four p.m. I was on my way to work that morning to thank him for that.

When Tim died, he had left us well taken care of. His life assurance policy had paid off the mortgage on our house and had made sure that university fees would never be a worry for Addison. It would never replace my husband, but it comforted me to know he had thought about how to take care of us when he wasn't here anymore long before he knew he was even sick.

I knocked on Aiden's door and entered. I smiled, set his routine coffee and muffin on his desk, and waited with my tablet to go over his diary as usual.

"Thanks, Ellis. I needed this!" He smiled and took a mouthful of coffee. He leaned back in his chair, rubbing his eyes, looking like he hadn't slept at all.

"Rough night?" I was being a little nosy and more informal than usual, but it seemed like an ear was just what he needed.

He glared at me, and I realised I had been lulled into a false sense of security with his smile and thank you. "Not that it's any of your business, but I was up looking at the surveys that have come back on the forty-three JLC Holdings properties."

His curt reply was like a slap in the face. "Anything I need to follow up on?" I knew if he had found anything, he would want me to chase up on estimates for repairs, potential problems that might occur, and any other factors that might arise.

"Not that I've found so far. I still have fourteen to look over, but at the minute, there's nothing that really puts me off. I have a report for you. It's mostly just maintenance work rather than anything major, so if you can get prices from the usual people. Also, we're going to need to start looking for three new property managers. We still haven't found anyone for Jim's properties, and there have been grumbles about being overstretched from the other three managers who are sharing the responsibility for his area."

I took notes on everything he mentioned. I would start chasing this up the second I left his office.

"When is the next meeting with JLC?" he asked.

"Thursday morning at ten."

He nodded and drank more coffee. "Who is sitting in on that one?"

I tapped the calendar app. "This is the one with Alan Jenkins and Everett Lowell."

He groaned. "Good old J and L themselves. *Fabulous.*" Sarcasm dripped off the last word. I smirked. The owners of JLC had a reputation of their own. They hated each other but made far too much money together to ever part ways, so meetings with them were usually unproductive and infuriating. "I think that's one of the days we should have nothing else scheduled after it. We'll need a drink afterwards. Book a table somewhere for lunch for both of us. We'll call it a reward for surviving Jenkins and Lowell."

I was caught a little by surprise. "Both of us?"

He looked at me with an intense stare. "Yes. I would like to reward my assistant for doing a good job. Is that okay with you?"

There it was again, that predatory look. Fuck, I wanted to be his prey. I held his stare. "That's more than okay with me."

"Well, I think that will do the both of us for now. See what you can do." He nodded, and I knew that was my cue to leave. "Oh, Mr Monroe?" I turned to look at him. "Thank you for calling Liz and asking her to pay me what you have. I really appreciate it."

He smiled at me. A beautiful, full, beaming grin. "You're very welcome."

I nodded and headed back to my desk, in awe of the beauty of his smile when it reached his eyes.

Chapter Seven
Aiden

"I APPRECIATE YOUR CONCERNS HERE, Aiden, but I really don't think this is getting anywhere." Alan Jenkins cast the contract to the conference room table and stared at me.

"I don't think your attitude is helping his much either, Alan," his partner, Everett Lowell, scolded.

I rolled my eyes and sighed. "Gentlemen, you are looking to offload forty-three properties. I have been through the surveys on every one of them, as has my assistant here. Munroe Holdings didn't get to where it is now by taking on properties that need as much work as four of your properties do at the price you're currently asking for them."

Everett nodded in agreement.

Alan shook his head.

I looked at Ellis, and I could see he understood now why they had the reputation they did. In fact, I think he was realising that it was like refereeing children in a playground. They were positively unbearable.

"Alan, Everett, I know you want the best price you can get. We are all businessmen here, but I also know that the best price for those properties is around ten percent less than where you have them priced. It's just how the market works. They will need extensive modernisation. You have the images taken inside them. You can see they look like the 1970s threw up inside them. They haven't been touched in over forty years."

I waited. They had been there since ten that morning. It was now almost two in the afternoon, and we still hadn't moved off the price to discuss any of the other items on the agenda. I was done with this bullshit. I wanted to take Ellis out on that lunch I had promised and forget about the rest of the day.

"I don't think we're going to get anywhere on this today." Everett spoke finally. Alan tutted and sighed disapprovingly.

I nodded. "I think you're right. Can I suggest that we reconvene next week at your earliest convenience, and we'll sort out the rest of the items on the agenda?"

Both men mumbled their agreement and started to pack up their belongings. Ellis pressed the intercom and called in one of the girls from the floor to escort the gentlemen to the lobby.

As soon as they were out of sight and earshot, I flopped into my chair, wringing my hands in my hair. "Jesus fucking Christ."

Ellis snorted a chuckle. "I wouldn't have believed it had I not seen it with my own eyes."

"They're fucking insane, aren't they?" I laughed.

Ellis nodded. "How do you ever get anything done with them?"

I shrugged. "I don't. I hold the meetings, listen to them disagree, and then do whatever the fuck I want with their juniors, who know how to handle them, because they never refuse a good enough deal. We'll get the properties, and at the discount I'm asking for, but not before we've been through this ridiculous ritual of umpiring their disagreements."

Ellis shook his head in disbelief.

"I don't know about you, Ellis, but I'm ready for a beer. Let's get the fuck out of here for a while." I smiled, and he smiled back. We gathered our paperwork, dropped it on our respective desks, and left the office for lunch.

I laughed when we arrived at the restaurant. "Here?"

There was a cheeky glint in his eyes that was beyond sexy. "You don't like Japanese food?"

I grinned and nodded. "I love Japanese food. In fact, I love coming here. I'm just surprised you didn't book somewhere fancy or expensive. Previous assistants have."

"Sure, I could have booked something like Oblix, but this place is much more me."

I smiled at him, biting back what I wanted to say to him. What I wanted to do. He was beautiful. He was unique and genuine. He was utterly kissable, and I would have happily defied my father and put my wants before the business needs for a man like Ellis.

"Earth to Aiden?" He nudged me playfully in the arm and nodded to the door he was holding open for me. I looked at him, and for a split second, there was a moment between us. I could see attraction from him, and I certainly felt it towards him. I cleared my throat, momentarily broke the spell, and walked in.

. . .

We were seated in just a few minutes, and a couple of ice-cold *Lucky Buddhas* were soon in front of us. I took a long swig from the bottle set in front of me. "Damn, I needed that," I said, setting the drink back down.

Ellis smirked and took a drink from his. I found myself transfixed at the way his lips kissed at the rim, thinking about things I could get them to kiss in a similar way. Ellis set his beer down and raised an eyebrow. *Busted. Again. Fuck.* I smiled and looked away, trying to act cooler than the beers in front of us.

"So, how long have you been an assistant?" I tried to change the atmosphere to something more bright and breezy instead of wanton and lust-fuelled, as I'm sure Ellis knew the looks I was giving him were.

"Oh, I would say about eight years now. I had a few years' permanent position, and then some things happened in my personal life, and I needed a little time off. These days, I like temping. I like moving around to different companies, getting experience of different office dynamics."

Something tightened in my chest when he said something happened in his personal life. But from the look on his face, I wasn't sure if I wanted to pry. I wasn't sure it was my place either. I was just his boss.

"And then you pulled the short straw and ended up working for me." I laughed.

"Oh, now that I did as a favour for my friend in the agency. Your reputation precedes you." He laughed, and I couldn't help but roll my eyes.

"Oh, I'm sure it does." I smirked. "I know all about what they say about me, and the secret Facebook groups they say it in."

Ellis blushed.

I grinned more. "Do I take it from the rosy glow you've now got on your cheeks that you're in said group?"

"Maybe."

I shrugged. "I've been a tyrant, but so was my father, and his father before him."

Ellis nodded. "After my experiences in Munroe Holdings and today's meeting, I can understand why there is a need for you to stand your ground so fiercely."

Did he really understand?

"It's a family business. I've been very fortunate to be born into that kind of family wealth, but it has its pitfalls. I have to sacrifice a part of me to be where I am today, and I guess sometimes that pisses me off and I take it out on the people who don't deserve it." He looked at me curiously, like he was about to ask what I had to sacrifice. Fortunately for me, the waitress arrived and interrupted that thread of conversation.

"That looks amazing. I might have to try it next time," Ellis said, his eyes on my food.

Without thinking about it, I lifted my chopsticks, grabbed some of the teriyaki sirloin steak soba from my plate, and offered it directly to Ellis' mouth. He looked right at me, opened his mouth, and accepted the food. A low hum of approval at the tastes rumbled through him, and my cock stirred. *Fuck.*

"That is delicious." He smiled.

"Yes, it is." I stared back.

Chapter Eight
Ellis

Damn, if he kept looking at me like that, I was going to end up spontaneously combusting. I didn't think about it, I just kept looking at him as I opened my mouth and let him offer me the food. The scene was ridiculously erotic, full of lust and intent, and made me once again look at Aiden as more than my boss.

"That is delicious," I managed to say, half scared that my mouth would engage before my brain and 'you are delicious' would fall out.

"Yes, it is." His eyes fixed on me, and if he was any other man, I would have been inclined to reply with flirting and sass and see where it would lead. But this was Aiden Munroe. My boss, a hard ass, not someone I should be casually flirting with. Hell, I still wasn't convinced the man was even gay. I kept convincing myself that it was just his power I was attracted to, and he wasn't really flirting with me, it was just that he was so used to using that power to influence people.

I broke the steady gaze between us by taking a long sip

of my beer and lifting my fork to get stuck in to my teriyaki chicken don buri.

———

The afternoon passed with idle chit-chat about work. How I was finding it, if I was happy enough to stay on for another three months, if I would consider becoming a permanent member of staff. A few more beers were consumed, and after about two hours and some cheesecake, we decided to head back to the office.

The chatter continued as we strolled the short distance back through the streets of the City of London until we reached the office.

"Can you grab those contracts and the information on the four properties we have the query with and come into the office, please?"

I agreed and headed into his office a few minutes later with everything he asked for.

"Take a seat." Aiden gestured to the sofa and coffee table in the corner of his large office. He grabbed papers of his own and sat beside me, lounging back over the seat.

"I don't know about you, but I'm already thinking this has been a very long day." His head was back, his eyes were closed, and his hand was over his face.

I couldn't help but agree. It felt like it should be home time already. Four hours in the company of Jenkins and Lowell had me feeling like I had been at work for a full eight hours.

"Don't worry. I'll try not to keep us here much longer than we need to be today. But we will need to work late tomorrow and next week, if that's okay with you?"

He asked me?

"I don't mind at all, but thanks for asking rather than assuming."

He looked right at me. *Shit.* Had the few beers I had had at lunch made my lips a little too loose?

"I don't ask often enough, do I? You might have plans."

Is he asking? "No. No plans beyond getting home after a long day." I don't know why I didn't mention Addison and Sylvie, but it just didn't seem like the right time. I didn't know if he was actually interested in me. I didn't know if he wanted to be with someone with a child even if he *was* interested in me. I looked right at him and tried to figure out if there could possibly be a reason behind it.

Suddenly, the air was charged with electricity. He kept my gaze, and I couldn't stop myself returning the look. It had been a while, but I recognised what this felt like. Any moment, one of us was going to lean in and kiss the other. I held my breath and waited for him to make a move.

Knock! Knock! Knock!

He sighed and looked away. "Come in!"

One of the girls on the floor came in to deliver the messages that had been gathering since we were out to lunch. "Your messages, Mr Munroe." She smiled and handed them over, completely blanking me. I didn't even exist in the room compared to Aiden. I couldn't help the smirk that formed on my face.

He took the pieces of paper from her, and curtly replied, "Thanks. You can go now."

Her smile didn't fade. She nodded and retreated out of the office.

His eyes fell back on me. "Stop that."

I couldn't help it. A chuckle erupted from me. "Sorry!"

He rolled his eyes and glared. "It's not funny. I hate that."

"What, being handsome and admired by all?"

He glared more, but there was a slight pull at the corner of his mouth. He was biting back a smile.

"It's a terrible hardship, I'm sure."

"Oh, like you wouldn't know what it's like to be gorgeous and admired." He laughed, looking at me with that look I loved. I watched the expression on his face change as he realised what he'd said. He clearly regretted it. He had given a hint of himself away. He was interested in me.

"How about we call this a day?" He stood up and moved away from me. And just like that, the moment was over. He wouldn't even look in my direction. This man was beyond infuriating.

Chapter Nine
Aiden

I was a bastard.

I had been comfortable with him, and I'd said he was gorgeous, and then I backpedalled like a complete spineless prick. I had dismissed him without even looking at him. The truth was, I was terrified. I'd had boyfriends in the past, but nothing was serious. Nothing gave me the feeling in my guts that I had when I looked at Ellis. My family life was difficult, and I wasn't sure I could try to explain that to him. I also didn't think I would want to hide Ellis from the world like I had with the other men in my past.

My phone interrupted my mental rambling.

"Hello?"

"Ade, it's me." My sister, Jennie.

"Hello, brat. What's up?" I grinned and waited for her.

She sighed. "You're such an asshole. I'm outside your door. Come let me in!" I snorted and hung up, heading for the front door.

I gave her a hug when she got inside. "Hello, you," I said into her hair as I squeezed her tight. "To what do I owe the pleasure?"

She kissed me on the cheek. "Just happened to be passing."

Yeah, right. I didn't believe that for a second. "Try again?"

"Okay. Mum said you sounded like shit the last time she spoke to you and she knew you wouldn't talk to her."

"She was right, but what makes her think I'll talk to you?"

Jennie punched me in the arm and headed straight for my kitchen to put the kettle on. She moved around the room, getting the cups, the milk, the teabags. She kept silent the whole time, and I sighed, knowing the game she was playing. She said nothing, and I eventually caved in and told her what she wanted to hear.

"Fine." I sighed.

She smirked. "It's clearly a guy. So, spill."

"Does it have to be about a man?"

Again, she gave me a look, and I admitted defeat.

"Okay! It's about a guy."

She smiled and went back to making the tea.

"He's a temp. He came to my office to work as my assistant. He's gorgeous, and I'm pretty sure he's gay too."

She spun around and stared. "You haven't asked him?"

I laughed and started to pour the milk into my mug. "How the fuck would that work, Jennie? Come on. Gay men are meant to have gaydar and just know if a person is gay or not. I don't have that shit. Maybe it's because I'm too repressed in my own sexuality, but I don't fucking know."

Jennie put her hand on my shoulder. "Relax. I still don't agree with Dad on this one. It's got you all tied in knots, and you clearly really like this guy. What's he called?" Her smile was comforting, and I did relax a little.

"Ellis Baxter."

"Ohh! Good name! A strong name."

"He strikes me as a strong man." I thought about Ellis, and about the fact that my attempting to keep my distance from him had only served to stop me from actually getting to know anything concrete about the man I worked with.

Jennie could read me like a book. There are just eighteen months between us, and while I was always the stable one, my sister was a flight of fancy kind of person. She let her instincts and her heart lead her, and for her, it worked. For me, I wasn't sure it would have made any kind of difference to how I was and how I was perceived to be.

"You'll get to know him, you know? You've realised it now and you'll make the effort."

I covered her hand on my arm and gave it a gentle squeeze. "I love you, Jen." There was nothing else I could say aside from that to truly express how grateful I was to have her as my sibling, or for the support, love, and understanding she offered me. "You've dated more than me. How do I get to know him without it feeling forced or like I'm prying?"

She lifted her mug of tea and walked into my living room, sat on the sofa, and thought about her words before she spoke. For the next hour, my kid sister schooled me in the finer points of getting to know another human being, and how not to come across as a massive arsehole.

I listened to everything my sister said, and when I was next in the office, I wanted to put it into play, but I just couldn't figure out a way to casually chat with Ellis. My palms got sweaty, my tongue got tied, and I started to revert to being a wanker, purely because that was what I was most used to being and most comfortable as. She texted that evening to ask how I was getting on and if I had got to know him any better.

I'm a failure. I texted back.

Have a little faith in yourself. You've been such a monumental prick for so long. It can be hard to teach an old dog new tricks. Keep at it. You can do it!

I chuckled and shook my head. Only my sister could be supportive and insulting all in one message.

Ellis was pushing me farther and farther out of my comfort zone. He was the kind of man to make me want more. He was also the kind of man who inspired me to want to be more. To do the things I had always dreamed of. To tell my father that my sexuality wasn't a business mistake, that it's just who I am, and not only am I proud of it, but it makes me the businessman with the loyalty to my family that I am.

I lifted my phone and buzzed through to Ellis's desk.

"Can you stay late tonight? I have some things I need your help with. I'll feed us." I waited for his reply. "Thank you. I'm sending you an email outlining the work for tonight and the prep I need for it. Also, there's a new meeting at half four. I have a representative of JLC coming in before we meet again with those assholes at the end of the week." He laughed, told me it was no problem, and hung up.

The sound of his laughter echoed in my head. I wasn't sure there was any part of that man I wasn't enjoying being around. His laughter was delightful.

By nine-thirty that night, there was a Chinese takeaway spread across the coffee table in my office, and Ellis and I were making the most of it and the cold beers I'd had delivered too. More and more, the chatter drifted from the job to general exchanging of information between two people who were trying to be more like friends than employees.

"Looking forward to another meeting with Jenkins and Lowell?" I grinned.

Ellis grimaced. "Can we have the rest of the day off again afterwards?"

"Unfortunately, no. If only. They're a pair of draining bastards."

He groaned, and his head fell back to rest on the cushion of the sofa. There was something about that sound. Something about the look on his face. All sense left me, and I leaned over and coupled my mouth with his. I cupped the side of his face and licked my tongue along the seam of his lips, begging him to part them.

His fingers found their way to the hair at the nape of my neck. His lips opened, his tongue duelled with mine, and I moaned against his mouth. Lust and a rampant need took over us both, and the sexual chemistry that had been brewing over the last few weeks exploded. I pressed myself against him. His hand went for the bottom of my shirt, pulling it free from my trousers, allowing him to slide his hand underneath it and touch my bare skin.

I moved back, bringing him with me so I could have him lying back on the sofa. I positioned myself between his legs, feeling his hard cock pressed against me and hungrily devouring him with my mouth. He pulled me hard against him, both hands under my shirt, grabbing my skin.

Needing me closer.

All I could think about was how much I craved him naked, how I wanted to be naked with him, and how much I desired to be inside him. I needed Ellis more than I had ever needed any man in my entire life, and every ounce of that feeling poured out of me into him via our lips.

Chapter Ten
Ellis

THE SECOND HIS lips touched mine, every nerve in my body was set on fire. I pulled him against me. I matched his ferocity with my own. I needed my hands on his skin, and I pulled his shirt free from his trousers to make sure I could get the contact I craved.

When he moved me down the sofa, I let him. I needed to feel him on top of me, pressed against me. I wasn't disappointed when he did. The warmth of his body on mine and the feeling of his rock-hard cock pressed against my stomach had my sensations overloaded.

I kissed him back hard. I touched his skin roughly, grabbing at him, needing him to be closer, knowing he wouldn't be close enough until he was inside me.

"Fuck, Aiden," slipped from my lips when his mouth moved to my neck. I moaned, grinding my hips against his, desperately craving more.

I hadn't been with a man since my husband died. Not a kiss, not a date, and certainly not a fuck. I wanted it all from Aiden, and I wasn't embarrassed to admit that I would happily take it now if he wanted to give it.

I felt one of his hands undoing my buttons as his mouth settled back on mine. I moaned into his kiss when his hand finally came into contact with my bare skin. He kissed over my jawline, my neck, and my now exposed chest. When his mouth enclosed my left nipple, my cock throbbed, begging for attention. He felt it too, because a moment later, his hand cupped my cock through my trousers, rubbing my length, making me moan like a horny schoolboy.

Jesus Christ. If he kept this up, I was going to come all over my boxers. His mouth moved over my skin, heading to my stomach. He palmed my cock harder, and my hips instinctively moved up against his hand, looking for more. His mouth teased my stomach, and his hand moved against my waistband.

Suddenly, I panicked. All I could think about was Tim, and how no one had touched me since him. I pushed at him, scrambling out from under him and hitting the floor with a thud.

"I can't!" anxiety overwhelmed my body. "I'm sorry." pusing away from him, I pulled myself off the floor and started to button up my shirt.

"Ellis," he pleaded.

I couldn't look at him. It would only lead to giving in, to doing what I was craving. We would keep going wherever this was going, and the only thought that was swimming in my brain at that moment was that I was cheating on my husband. My dead husband.

"I'm so sorry," I blurted, and fled, grabbing my coat and bag and not even waiting for the lift. I bolted down the fire stairs, down all six floors, and out onto the street. I didn't stop sprinting until I was two streets away and hailed a London cab.

What the hell was I doing?

"Hello, son." Sylvie smiled when I walked into the living room. "What's wrong?" She read the expression on my face far too well.

I flopped onto the sofa beside her. "It's nothing."

She raised her eyebrow at me. She wasn't buying it, and I didn't blame her. I wasn't exactly convincing. "Are you going to tell me?"

"We kissed." I winced, blurting it out. I felt like a cheater. I felt like I was betraying her and the memory of her son. That feeling had lifted me out of Aiden's office and into a cab home.

"You kissed Aiden?"

I nodded. "Well, he kissed me, but yes."

Sylvie got giddy with a big grin on her face. "Oh my God. Darling, that's brilliant! What's he like? Is he a good kisser? Did it turn you on? Could you feel it in your toes?"

I looked at her with my mouth open.

"What? You thought I would be angry?" She patted my arm.

I shrugged. "I'm angry with myself. It's like I'm saying Tim didn't matter to me."

Sylvie rolled her eyes and looked at me. "Do you think my son was the kind of man who would have wanted to see anyone he loved hurt or miserable?"

I shook my head. That was as far from anything Tim would have wanted could possibly be. "God, no."

"Well, Ellis, he loved the bloody bones of you, so why would you be any different?" She shook her head at me. "He wouldn't want you to be miserable for the rest of your life. You're still so young, my darling, and I know Tim died, but you didn't. You owe it to him and to yourself to have a life and enjoy it and live it to the fullest." Sylvie hugged me hard. "Now, answer the damn question. Is he a good kisser?"

I smiled and held her tight to me, kissing her cheek. "I love you, Sylvie."

"I love you too, son. And so did Tim." She paused. She stared. "AND?" she asked again.

I laughed. "You're terrible, Muriel." She slapped my thigh, and I admitted defeat. "Okay! Okay! Yes! Yes, he was a damn good kisser, and I felt it everywhere."

She clapped her hands like an excited child. "And?"

"And what?"

"Are you going to see him again?"

"Well, I work with him, Sylvie. I think it's highly possible I'll lay eyes on him again."

Again, she slapped my thigh.

"Jesus, okay, bully! I don't know. He's got a habit of blowing hot and cold, so I really don't know what the fuck to expect when I get back into work in the morning. And anyway, I fucked it all up, didn't I?"

She stared, silently asking me to clarify.

"It was good, and I got hot for him, and it was going a certain way, and then I fucked it all up by freaking out and running away."

Sylvie bit her lip and pity filled her features.

"All I could think of was the last person I was ever with that like that was Tim, and I just couldn't do it."

She nodded. "Sweetheart, I get it. The first time I was with someone after Tim's dad left us was hard as hell. And he was a wanker. Had I been still mourning the loss of a decent man, I might have had the same reaction. He'll forgive you. You just need to explain, and if he lets you slip through his fingers after all that, well then, he's a damn idiot and you can tell him I said that." She waggled her finger at me.

I laughed at her again. "You know, I've actually started to like this job. I'm not sure that threatening him with you is going to let me keep it. Nor is my behaviour tonight."

Sylvie glared, and I walked away before she had a chance to wallop my thigh again. "I need a bath. Night, gorgeous." I laughed.

"Brat!" she shouted up the stairs after me.

Chapter Eleven
Aiden

I TOSSED and turned all night. I replayed what had happened in my head over and over. I tortured myself with how good it felt to touch him. How good he smelled. How good he tasted. I thought about what it would have been like to have taken things further with him. My cock was rock-hard and throbbed in need of attention, but it felt pathetic to help myself out like that when he wasn't there.

He had rejected me. Things had been going so well. He had kissed me back. When he pressed his body against mine, it certainly felt like he was enjoying it as much as I was. I didn't understand what had happened. One minute, lust had a passionate hold over both of us, and then, suddenly, he was off the sofa, pulling himself back together and running out the door as fast as his damn legs would carry him.

I replayed every moment. Had I overstepped a boundary? Had I moved too fast for him? Had I almost discovered he had the ugliest cock on the planet?

I thought about asking my sister for advice but quickly

dismissed the idea. I wasn't sure I could stick the fact that she would take the piss and pass remarks on my technique.

I finally decided that perhaps I should just take it as a sign from the universe that it wasn't meant to be. Maybe I was better off without the prospect of a potential sexual harassment lawsuit looming over me.

I finally settled myself into a restless sleep, but I couldn't quite shake the feeling that this was karma paying me back for not standing up to my father and being open and honest about everything in my life publicly.

My coffee and muffin were on my desk when I arrived late, but Ellis was nowhere to be seen. My heart sank. I had all but convinced myself to tell him it was a mistake, and I was sorry, but there was still that part of me that wanted him to say sorry about what happened and explain. I guessed that wasn't about to happen. I resigned myself to my fate and got stuck in to my work. I'd apologise for overstepping the boss/employee line with him later.

It was about twenty minutes later that there was finally a knock at my door, and Ellis appeared around it. "Your daily schedule?"

"Yes. Come on in and close the door."

He nodded and did as I asked.

"Look," I started, "before we start, I just wanted to say sorry about last night."

"You have nothing to be sorry about..." he interrupted, but I didn't want to hear the platitudes. I didn't want it to be some awkward bullshit.

"No, just let me say this."

"But, I..."

"Please!" I insisted. There was nothing he could possibly say that would make me feel any better about all this. "I'm sorry about what happened last night. I really don't know what came over me. I am your employer, and you are my employee. That is a line that should never be crossed, and I very much overstepped it last night. I would like to apologise, and I understand completely if you wish to file a complaint with HR about it. Hell, you are perfectly within your rights to take me to a tribunal for sexual harassment." I couldn't look at him. My resolve would break, I would beg him to give me another chance, and my career and business would be in ruins. No matter what I wanted, I wouldn't let anything happen to the company that had been in my family for so long.

"Okay," he replied flatly. "Although, I want you to know that I will not be taking it to HR or any tribunal."

I glanced up at him. His eyes were cold, his face emotionless. "Thank you." I cleared my throat. "Now, can we get back to normal?"

"Sure," he mumbled, then started to go through the diary for the day ahead.

Chapter Twelve
Ellis

I couldn't believe it. I was going to tell him why I ran. I was going to apologise. I wouldn't have given him every gory detail, but enough to make him understand. Instead, Aiden made it very clear that it was a mistake he regretted. A mistake he was worried about causing scandal to his company. It wasn't even fair to call it disappointment. It was so much more. I cursed myself for making such a mess of things. I should have stayed and had a bit more courage about it. It had been hard. No one had been able to even remotely create a glimmer of passion in me since Tim. Friends had given up pushing available attractive men in my direction, knowing full well that there was nothing they could do to spark any interest in me for them.

And then I walked into his office that first morning, and I met Aiden Munroe. I didn't see it then, but it had become more apparent to me as time went on. I was instantly attracted to him, and as more than a picture-perfect man. There was something about how he carried himself, and the respect he had for his family as I came to find out later, that really spoke to me of the quality of the man beneath the gorgeous exterior.

But then he went and ruined it all, and my sense of disappointment over it ran a lot deeper than I realised it would. I stood there, shell-shocked, listening to him tell me that I had every right to go to HR and complain. That I had every right to take him to an employment tribunal and ruin him with a sexual harassment case. All I had wanted to do was explain myself and try to get back to what had happened the night before to see where that would have gone.

I ran through his schedule for the day and left his office. He barely looked at me the entire time, and I felt like some cheap little blemish that needed to be dealt with as soon as possible. I sat at my desk and thought about calling Liz and telling her she needed to find someone else to fill the position, but then I remembered something Tim used to tell me about giving up when I had a really bad day at work. *Nothing worth having ever came easy.* I wondered if that applied to Aiden as well.

Things settled back into their same routine, and I started to feel not as humiliated as I had. Not perfect, but far from a disaster worth quitting over. My mobile rang, and I saw Sylvie's name on the screen. "What's wrong?"

"Jesus, son. Why does anything have to be wrong?"

"Sorry. It doesn't."

She sighed. "I take it I need to come down there and slap someone's fine arse for you? I will, you know?"

She meant it too. It cheered me up to hear someone so willing to fight my battles for me. "Will you put the daggers away, woman?" I laughed. "I'm a big boy. I'll live. Now, what did you want?"

She laughed back. "Not too big for me to take over my knee for cheek. Anyway, you know that lovely fella, Rodney?"

I thought about which profile pic had been Rodney's. Decent-looking bloke from what I remembered, and he seemed to be a gentleman too. I knew she'd been out to coffee with him and all had gone well.

"I remember him," I answered.

"Well, he's asked me out on Thursday night, and I've accepted. But that means you have no one to keep Addison if you need to work late, and I thought, since you have been, I should give you a heads up, so you know you can't that night."

"Not a problem. I wouldn't want to be the reason you didn't get your end away with some older piece of ass, now, would I?"

She howled with laughter. "I'm telling you now, son, you're in trouble when you get home. Now, go and do some bloody work."

I shook my head and laughed. "Love you."

"Love you too, Ellis. See you when you get home. I'm making your favourite tea tonight."

I didn't have a chance to reply. She had already hung up, so I couldn't argue with her. *Sly old bag.*

***

"So, are you going to tell me what happened with him or not?" She was staring. I knew I wasn't going to get away with not telling her. *Bloody infuriating woman.*

I sighed. "I don't know where to start. I was going to go

in and tell him I was sorry, and why I needed to run and hope he would understand. But he just kept talking over me and not letting me get a bloody word in, so there wasn't much point in trying."

"So, what exactly did the silly bugger say?"

I explained everything he said. The comments about going to human resources and tribunals, and all of it. When I was done, Sylvie just stared at me.

"Are you stupid?" she asked.

What the fuck?

I stammered. "What? Where did that come from?"

"Honestly, you have so much to learn for a man who has been married and has a child of his own. He's panicking. I think he likes you too, but he's a rich and powerful man and, sweetheart, you gave his ego one hell of a kicking. He's probably not used to that at all. Powerful men get what they want. He wanted you. You didn't give it to him."

I shook my head.

"Ellis, don't shake your head at me. I am your mother-in-law. I know how the world works. Not to burst your little bubble, but my Tim wasn't exactly a virgin when you and he got together." She laughed, and I sighed a laugh in reply, shaking my head.

"I know. But..."

"But you're a bit like him, and his need to push you away has bruised your pride, just like you bruised his."

I couldn't argue with her. She was too damn smart for her own good, and I was defeated.

"So, what do I do?"

"Oh, that's easy, my lovely boy. You just keep being you. He'll come around eventually." She nodded at me, patted my hand, and got up off the sofa. "Now, I'm off to Skype with Rodney in my room."

"No video sex, lady. This is a family household."

She gave me the middle finger and walked out of the room as I sat laughing.

Chapter Thirteen
Aiden

I DON'T KNOW what happened when Ellis went home the night before, but the next morning, he was bright, breezy, and back to his usual self. I was more than a little relieved and a lot happier to see it. I needed him to be the same around me as he had always been. I wanted it that way. Even if it was torturous to not have him the way I wanted. I convinced myself that I would be happy just having him around, smiling, joking, and flirting, just like he had been.

The acquisition of the JLC properties was eating up almost all of our day, and the back and forth between their people and ours was getting ridiculous.

"This is never-ending." He sighed in frustration at the end of the day.

I puffed out my cheeks, exasperated. "I swear, had I known it was going to be this much of a headache, I don't think I would have bothered."

Ellis smiled.

"Honestly. I've dealt with them before, and yes, they are wankers, and they are difficult, but nothing has ever been like this. I know the company, and I know these properties.

They didn't have them for very long. They bought them on a whim in an auction that happened about a year ago. I saw them myself, but they were in such a state that I was never going to waste money on them by getting them back up to scratch. They've tried to paper over the cracks and do it all on the cheap, and it's showing on the surveys that have been done."

"Are they being cowboys?"

I shook my head. "Not intentionally. They just bit off more than they could chew on these properties. Easy enough done when you keep trying to outdo your partner. Alan bought them, and Everett hasn't been interested in fixing them up. Now, Everett is pushing for them to be sold on. Alan thinks he's got to prove a profit can be made, and Everett just doesn't give a fuck as long as they're ditched."

He nodded. I liked his interest in the dealings of the company, but more so, I liked that he never hesitated to ask me, and was more than happy to sit listening to me ramble on about the business.

"Are you sure you wouldn't like to be more than an assistant in a company like this?" I offered. "We have an entry program. I could talk nicely to the boss for you and pull a few strings if you wanted in."

He shook his head. "I like this work, but I also like the freedom of temping. Gives me time to myself when I need it. It's been invaluable in the past." The smile faded from his face, and I wondered what had made him sad. I wondered what had taken up his time so completely that temping was a consideration for him.

I glanced over at the clock. "Shit. It's past six-thirty. You can head out if you like. I think we've wrestled with the JLC mess for long enough today. I need a drink and dinner with my sister."

"Thanks. I could do with a soak in the bath." He smiled. I tried not to think of him in the bath and nodded with a stifled smile in reply.

"See you tomorrow, Ellis."

"Night, Aiden." He got up and walked out of the conference room. I waited before I moved. I texted my sister and got up to leave myself.

Don't hate me, but I need a rain check. I've been dealing with Alan and Everett's shit at work, and I am fucked.

It wasn't long before my phone pinged in reply.

As long as you promise to update me on Operation Getting To Know Ellis.

I winced. I hadn't told her what had happened. Where would I start. Feelings of guilt and misunderstanding flooded me; I had been such an idiot.

Chapter Fourteen
Ellis

Aiden's face appeared around the doorframe of his office.

"I know it's really short notice, but is there any way you can work tonight?" I looked at him, and I knew he could read my expression. "Look, if you can't tonight, it's fine, but it would mean I need you in at the weekend."

Damn. The weekend was my time with Addison, and I wasn't about to give that up. I was away from her enough during the week in this job as it was.

I sighed. "I'll have to sort some things, but yes. I can be here tonight if you need me to be."

Aiden smiled, thanked me, and disappeared back into his office. I lifted my phone and called Sylvie's mobile.

"Hi, it's me. I have to work tonight. I know you've got your date and I don't want you to miss out on it."

"Well, then, what do you want me to do?"

"Can you drop her off with me here on the way? Pack her a blanket and some colouring stuff, and that bloody book. I'll sort something with her."

Sylvie agreed, and I hung up. *Fuck.* I didn't really need

to be having Addison at work. Things with Aiden were diffi-cult enough as it was, but I wasn't going to let Sylvie cancel her first chance at a date in months.

I'll text you when we're in the lobby x

I fired back a reply to say I would meet Sylvie there and asked what time she expected to arrive.

Aiden walked past. "Cancelling a date for tonight?" He smirked.

"Something like that." My cryptic reply clouded his expression, and he shot me a filthy side glance as he went back into his office.

Great. Just great.

"Daddy!" Addison ran towards me and jumped up into my arms. "I'm going to help you at work."

Sylvie laughed, handed me Addison's bag, and kissed us both on the cheek. "I can cancel this if you need me to."

I shook my head. "No way. She's my daughter, and I need to take care of her." I kissed Sylvie's cheek. "You look amazing, by the way. Isn't Nanna pretty tonight?"

Addison nodded. "She's going to meet a handsome prince and kiss him," she whispered.

Sylvie winked at her granddaughter. "Only if he's very handsome and rich."

I shook my head with a chuckle. "Come on, monster. Let's get you upstairs. And you..." I looked at Sylvie with a wink. "...Don't do anything I wouldn't do."

She laughed and started to walk out of the lobby and

back onto the London streets. "Don't wait up!" she called over her shoulder.

Addison squeezed me tighter, and I walked her to the lifts and up to my floor.

"You have to sit here and behave. And I need you to do some colouring in for me. It's very important work, and it would help me so much. Do you think you can do that?"

Addison nodded.

I pulled her colouring book and pencils from her backpack and set her up on the sofa and coffee table to the right of my desk. Usually, it was for clients waiting on Aiden, but since there was pretty much no one else around, I didn't think there would be much of an issue with her sitting there.

I sat at my desk and started to review the new reports on the four problem buildings again. JLC had sent in their own surveyors, and I needed to compare the report we commissioned with the report they had sent over.

Addison was brilliantly behaved. She worked away on her colouring like it was the most important task in the universe. Her little brow creased up, and she reminded me so much of Tim. He got the same look on his face when he had been concentrating on anything. Conflicting emotions washed over me. Pride in my beautiful little girl, and loss that her other father was no longer with us.

"Monster, I just have to go and get something. You be a very good girl and don't move from that sofa. Okay?"

Addison nodded her agreement. "Okay, Daddy."

I got up and headed down the corridor to the main printer/copier room for everything I had just printed out.

.   .   .

When I got back to my desk five minutes later. Addison was nowhere in sight. Dread filled every part of me.

FUCK!

Chapter Fifteen
Aiden

I WAS LOOKING over the reports JLC had sent over. I needed to find out what they were up to, and why I still hadn't got a deal on their properties yet. Ellis was at his desk, looking over them with a fine-tooth comb. I was in the conference room, needing the space to spread out the vast amount of paperwork this was creating.

When I looked up, a little girl with cute curls and pretty brown eyes was looking at me.

"Hello." She smiled.

"Hello."

"Have you seen my daddy?"

I shook my head. I didn't think we had anyone else working on the floor tonight aside from Ellis and me. "What's your name?"

"I am Addison Baxter," she said, punctuating every word with a little nod from her sweet head.

Baxter? Ellis? My heart sank. He was involved with a woman and had a child with her? "What's your daddy's name?" I hoped I was wrong. She couldn't really be Ellis's, could she?

"My daddy is called Ellis."

Shit. That hit me like a kick in the balls. Ellis had a child. And what's more, in all our little getting to know each other chats here and there, not once had he mentioned her. Was he in the closet? Was he bisexual? Or worse, was this some sort of messed up game from one of my leading competitors to see us ruined with scandal? God forgive me, but I needed to get information from this little girl.

"Where's your mummy?"

She looked sad. "I don't have one. I had two daddies, but Daddy Tim went to live in heaven with the other angels. I can't see him for a very long time."

Fuck. Now I felt like a complete asshole. Ellis had been with someone, loved him enough to have a child with him, and somehow, he was now dead, and Ellis was a single dad.

How did I ever read a situation so wrongly?

"Come sit with me." I gestured, and she cautiously walked into the room and around the table to me. I held out my hand for her to shake. "My name is Aiden, and I work with your daddy. It's very nice to meet you."

Addison grinned and shook my hand fiercely.

"Would you like to sit on my knee and draw me a picture?"

She nodded. I pulled her up onto my knee, gave her a blank page and my pen, and watched.

"What are you going to draw?"

Her little hand moved with the pen over the page. "I'm going to draw my daddy working at his computer." A form appeared; a large oval of a body, a similar oval for a head, a line out of the body on each side. Each line ended in a circle with five lines out of each.

"How old are you?" I asked as I watched.

"Four, but I'll be five in two weeks."

I grinned. She was adorable. "Well, I think you are an amazing artist for someone who is five in two weeks." She nodded in agreement and continued to draw a portrait of her father.

We sat there, chatting back and forth about the picture she was drawing and all the little details she was adding to it for some time. Eventually, I was aware of eyes watching us. Addison felt them too and looked up to find her dad standing in the doorway.

"Daddy!" She held up her drawing for him to see. "Look! It's you. Aiden says I'm a very good artist."

Ellis smiled. "You're a very good artist, monster, but I told you not to move from the sofa!"

The little girl looked up at me with a grin. "Oops."

Ellis and I both laughed at her reaction, and I caught his gaze and tried to let him know just how amazing I thought they both were in a single look. Something in his expression softened, and he came over to sit on the same side of the table as me and the adorable Addison.

He leaned over and kissed her. "Sorry about this." He looked at me.

"You should be for not telling me you have such a delightful daughter." I tickled her, and her giggles filled the room. Ellis beamed with pride when he looked at her, but I could see the touch of sadness when he did.

"It's complicated."

"She told me."

"Aiden asked where my mummy is, and I told him Daddy Tim is in heaven," Addison interrupted.

I looked at her in awe. So, that was what they meant when they said kids don't miss a thing.

"Oh, did you now?" Ellis mouthed 'sorry' to me over Addison's head. I just smiled.

"Daddy. Can Aiden read me *The Last Noo Noo?*"

I crinkled my forehead. *The who?*

Ellis smirked. "Yes, he can read your bedtime story, but only if he wants to, monster."

I gave her a little squeeze. "I would be honoured to read your bedtime story to you, Addison."

She slid herself off my knee and ran out of the room. "I'll go get it!" she called out as she disappeared.

"I'm sorry I never mentioned her."

"I get it. Life is complicated, for everyone. But she's adorable. Can I ask what happened?"

Ellis didn't get the chance to answer because Addison came barrelling back into the room with her favourite book. She slammed it on the table and Ellis pulled her onto his lap. I lifted the book, opened to the first page, and started to read to her about Marlon.

By the time I reached the end, Addison was asleep on her dad's lap. He smiled down at her. "That book never fails."

I sat there, awestruck, watching him snuggle the sleeping form on his knee. He kept his eyes on her as he started to softly speak.

"Tim was the love of my life. I met him when I was twenty." I stayed silent, wanting to know more. "Tim was athletic, smart. He was training to be a geography teacher back then. Not exciting, I know, but it meant the world to him. He wanted to make a difference. His dad had been like my own family. He didn't want a gay son, and he told his mother that it was him or Tim." Ellis laughed. "Sylvie told him that if he thought she would pick him over her beautiful boy, he had another think coming. He walked out the very next day. She's like a mother to me. I don't know where

I would be without her. She and this little thing are my world."

"What happened?"

"About three years ago, Tim got what he thought was just a chest infection. He was a teacher by then and schools are a breeding ground for germs. After about a month and a few courses of antibiotics, he still had this nasty cough that just wouldn't leave. He kept going back to the doctor, and eventually, after some CT scans, they told us that it was lung cancer. Stage three B, with a nine percent survival rate at the five-year mark. He had two masses on his left lung, and it had spread to his lymph nodes. He fought, he had chemo and surgery, but Tim passed away eight months later. Addison was just a baby, really."

I took his hand in mine and squeezed it. This man was outstandingly brave. He had lost the man he loved and was a single dad raising a gorgeous little girl. My heart fluttered in my chest to think of him in pain. All I wanted to do was comfort him.

"How did you get this pretty little girl?"

"We had a civil partnership in 2007 and did the whole marriage thing when this little one was about a year old. She's his. We had a surrogate, and we used Tim's sperm and a donor's egg, and next time..." His voice caught in this throat, and I put my other hand over his. "Next time it was going to be my sperm and a donor's egg. We planned for at least two."

I didn't know what to say after that. I was lost in a well of emotion of my own. I wanted to hold him. I wanted to be his comfort. I wanted to help him honour the memory of his husband and raise their little girl with him. I had never even remotely thought about anyone like this. Sure, I'd had boyfriends; usually men still in the closet who wouldn't blab about it all over London. Ellis had changed everything.

"I don't think we'll get much more done tonight with that little beauty lying there. Can I take you both home?"

Ellis shook his head. "It's fine. We'll just get the train."

I shook my head. "Aww, she's fast asleep. It wouldn't be fair to disturb her. Let me take you home."

Ellis nodded.

"Okay, just let me go and grab some things from my office and call the car to meet us downstairs."

"Thank you."

I smiled at him, feeling a pull towards him, and I headed for my office.

Chapter Sixteen
Ellis

HE WAS SO INCREDIBLY sweet with Addison, and when he held my hand, I felt the warmth of his skin spread a soothing feeling up my arm and across my whole body. There was definitely something about him. Sylvie was right. *I shouldn't be overthinking this too much. I should just let it go and see what happens.*

When we got to the kerb to get in the car, Aiden opened the door and revealed there was a child seat in the back. I didn't even know he would have considered such a thing, never mind having actually had one put in the car while we got ready for it to arrive.

"You have a car seat?"

"I had Derek collect one from the Argos in Cheapside on his way here with the car."

I was speechless. This was not the thoughtless bastard I had come to know from working with him. This was something else. I settled Addison in the seat and strapped her in. Derek handed the keys to Aiden and smiled. I got into the passenger side, and he got into the driver's side.

"All set?"

I glanced over at Addison, secure in her new seat, and she settled back into her deep sleep. "Looks like it."

He nodded. "So where am I heading?"

"Grove Road in Sutton."

Aiden tapped on the satnav and headed off into the evening London traffic.

The miles passed with idle chitchat, and I was, for the most part, grateful for it. I had shared so much with him, and I felt exposed. He still wasn't sharing too much of himself with me.

He pulled up into the driveway of my home, and he helped me get Addison into the house, carrying her from the car to her bedroom while I got our belongings and unlocked the front door. I quickly got Addison into her vest and pants and tucked her into bed.

When I got back to the living room, Aiden was looking at the family photos on the wall. I followed his eyes and saw the photo of Tim and me holding Addison when she was just born.

"She looks just like him," he said, without looking over his shoulder.

I agreed. "Can I get you a coffee?"

He looked over at me and nodded.

"Have a seat and make yourself at home. I'll be back shortly."

I watched him briefly as he slid his suit jacket down over his broad shoulders and back, took off his tie, and undid the buttons on his collar. I wanted to walk over to him and kiss him. Instead, I retreated to the kitchen to make coffee. I heard the TV switch on and the delightful sounds of Tom Ellis playing *Lucifer* coming from the living room.

"*Lucifer?*" I handed him a mug and took a seat on the sofa beside him.

"Yeah. Don't you watch it?" He took the cup from me and had a sip.

I laughed. "Oh, I watch it."

We sat there and chatted more about the kind of music and films and TV shows we enjoyed, and it turned out we had a lot of likes in common.

"Okay, this is the dealbreaker." He laughed. "*Star Trek*, or *Star Wars*?"

I paused like I was actually giving it some thought. "*Trek*, and I think Quinto makes a damn fine Spock."

Aiden's laughter filled the room, and goosebumps lifted on my skin. "Thank fuck for that!"

The chatter faded and so did the coffee, and there were a few pauses in the conversation that were loaded with sexual tension. It was palpable. I could feel that he was being pulled to me, and I felt pulled to him, but neither of us had the courage to breach the distance between us.

"Well, I guess I should head home." He made a move to get up and grabbed his tie and jacket. I stood and quietly walked with him to the door.

"Thank you for everything this evening." My eyes met his again, and he smiled broadly.

"Anytime. She's a pleasure. And so are you."

With that one comment, I was undone. Whatever had been stopping me previously now didn't exist. I took a single step forward, firmly into his personal space, and let my lips find his. I felt a jolt of surprise from him, disappearing as he returned my kiss. With everything that had been bubbling between us for weeks, I had expected this to be a passionate, hard kiss. Instead, it was a soft, loving, beautiful thing, evolved from mutual adoration and a knowledge that, after this, neither of us would ever be the same again.

His tongue swept over mine, his hands found their way

to my waist, and he pulled me tight against him as he worshipped me sweetly with his mouth. All too soon, it was over.

"I should get going."

Everything in me wanted to ask him to stay. Instead, I nodded and stood there watching as he got in his car and left, my lips still tingling with the touch of his.

Chapter Seventeen
Aiden

I WAS STILL FLOATING by the time I arrived home. It felt incredible to have him kiss me like that. I needed to talk to my sister.

"What the hell are you calling so late for?" she grumbled.

"He has a daughter. He had a husband. He kissed me."

"Wait... what? Slow down!" She chuckled.

"He was married. His husband got cancer and died. They had a surrogate, and they had a daughter, and she's five in two weeks."

"Okay. Are you okay with that?"

I didn't hesitate. "Yes."

"And he kissed you?"

I grinned. "Yes. I've never met anyone like him."

I heard her stifle a groan. "Oh my God, my brother is actually in love!"

Now it was my turn to groan. "It's not like that."

She didn't sound convinced. I wasn't sure I was either. She broke my train of thought with a question I had been avoiding thinking about. "What are you going to do about Dad?"

My father had old-fashioned thinking when it came to business. He thought my being openly gay would cause problems. He didn't think a homosexual CEO was something the business world would handle. He thought it would bring attention and scrutiny that wasn't necessary. In some respects, I agreed. I wanted my private life to stay private, and I didn't need people looking for scandal just because I'm gay. But, on the other hand, I hated it. I hated that I couldn't just be myself. I respected my father's wishes, though.

Jennie took my pause as a sign that I hadn't been thinking about that part. "Yeah, I wouldn't know what to do about it either. Well... I would, but I think you listen to Dad's thoughts on it a lot more than I would."

She had me gathering my thoughts about it now. "What if I don't want to with this?"

She gasped. "Holy shit, this must be serious!"

"Maybe," I told her. "I'm going to go and think about it."

"Sure. I'm happy for you, Aiden. I really am."

"Thanks, Jennie. Love you and talk to you later."

"Love you too." And she hung up.

I sat there in the relative darkness of my living room, thinking about everything that had happened that evening. What I felt about Ellis, what I felt about my father, and most of all, whether or not I thought Ellis was worth coming out to the world for. It reminded me of a song lyric from Snow Patrol, about if he was worth it or not, because if you had to think about it, then that was your answer. When I thought about whether Ellis was worth it, there was no hesitation in my mind. The man was perfect in my eyes, and worth anything I needed to do to keep him.

The next morning, I got into work earlier than usual. I had tossed and turned all night long. At around five, I admitted defeat and just went into the office.

I pulled out all the information I had to work on, but I just couldn't get around to doing any of the work. I paced the office so much I was pretty sure there was a track marked out in the carpet. I looked out the window. I sat and stared at my computer screen. All I could think of was Ellis.

Eventually, it was seven, and Ellis appeared at my door with coffee and a muffin, just as he did every morning now. I couldn't help but grin at the sight of him, and he smiled warmly in return.

"Can you close the door a minute?"

Ellis went back to the door and closed it. "Something wrong?"

I shook my head. "God, no! Actually, I have something I want to discuss with you."

His brow furrowed.

"It's about last night. Basically, I liked it, and I would like to do it more. You, and kissing you, and time with Addison."

A soft, affectionate smile spread across Ellis's face. "I would enjoy that a lot. I'm pretty sure Addison would too. She asked if you could come and read her a story again soon."

My heart leapt, and a grin spread across my face. I moved around my desk and into his space. He closed the gap between us, and unlike the night before, there was passion, hunger, and we pulled each other hard against one another. Grabbing, needing, our tongues duelling.

Ellis broke the kiss first. "Shit, we're at work!" He laughed.

"Mmm, we need to stop," I agreed, pressing my lips against his again, cupping his face in my hands.

He moaned against my mouth.

Dammit! I was in danger of locking the door to my office and not stopping with Ellis until he was screaming my name and everyone on this floor—hell, even the whole building—knew exactly what we were doing.

I pulled back and looked at him. "If we don't stop now, I won't stop until I'm inside you."

"Fuck." He groaned. I knew what he meant. Leaving him to get on with his work would be the hardest thing I had done in a while.

"Get out now, while you still can, and you need to pick somewhere for us to go on a date."

He grinned so damn seductively and raised an eyebrow. "Okay," he agreed, and walked out of my office. This was going to be the best kind of torture I had ever experienced in my life.

Chapter Eighteen
Ellis

A week later

"Addison says I have to invite you to her birthday party. But trust me, it's a bunch of screaming, sugar-loaded four and five-year-olds and a bouncy castle. I don't blame you if you don't want to go."

"I'd love to." He grinned. "When is it?"

I scrunched up my face. "Ahh, tomorrow."

"What time?"

"About two would be perfect."

He nodded. "I'll be there at eleven and give you a hand with all the preparation if that's any good for you?"

I could have kissed him. "Yes, please. That would be amazing. Sylvie and I always end up running around like headless chickens."

"Not a problem. At your place, I assume?"

"Oh, yes. At my house."

"I wouldn't miss it for the world."

There was nothing about this man that didn't surprise me. We had only just started going out together, and while he had met Addison already, I didn't think he would be interested in a child's birthday party. I was constantly being surprised by him. My phone started to ring on my desk, and I left his office to go and answer it.

There was a knock at the door at five minutes to eleven on Saturday morning. When I answered it, there stood Aiden with a huge bunch of balloons, a bunch of flowers, a large gift bag, and a good bottle of wine.

"What's all this?" I laughed when I saw him standing with his arms full.

"You can't come to a birthday party empty-handed; that would be impolite." He laughed back.

"Wine, Aiden? She's five."

"Har har. That's for you, but if you're going to be rude, I'll just give it to Sylvie."

As if by magic, at the sound of her name, my mother-in-law appeared.

"Did I hear my name being taken in vain?" she asked as she walked up to the door.

Aiden handed her the bunch of flowers. "Not in vain, I promise. These are for you. It's lovely to meet you."

I had to hand it to him; he was making a huge effort, and I really appreciated that. It couldn't have been easy to walk into the house and meet the mother-in-law of the man you're dating. Sylvie was a pussycat, but she was protective as hell. She had promised me she would be on her best behaviour, though.

"Welcome to the madhouse, Aiden. Lovely to meet you too. Come on in. I'll just put these somewhere they won't get run over by kids." She laughed and disappeared into the kitchen.

"Hello, you." Aiden smiled at me as he stood inside the doorway beside me. I grinned and leaned in to give him a soft yet quick kiss.

"Eww, Daddy! No kissing!" Addison called out from the top of the stairs. I watched as she looked over at Aiden, taking in the big gift bag and the balloons and running down the stairs towards us. "Is that for me?"

She was such a cheeky little monster.

"I dunno," Aiden said. "I think it might be a mistake. I heard someone was having a birthday party today, but I'm not sure what they were called. Madison, I think."

"Addison!" She giggled.

"Maybe it was Alison."

"Addison!" She squealed a little louder.

"Addison? No, I don't think that was the name."

"It's me!" She started to bounce up and down. "It's me! It's me!"

Aiden knelt down to her level and tapped his cheek. "Kiss here, Princess Addison, and you may have your gift." Addison threw her arms around Aiden's neck, kissed his cheek, and then stood with her hand out.

I shook my head and raised an eyebrow at her behaviour. She turned with her goodies and went to disappear off upstairs again. "Ah, monster. Are you forgetting something?" I asked her.

She turned to me and grinned. "Sorry, Daddy. Thank you, Aiden." She grinned and sprinted back upstairs as fast as she could carry her gifts.

"Thank you for spoiling her like that. You really didn't need to. I wasn't expecting you to."

Aiden smiled. "I know I didn't, but I wanted to make a good impression with everyone."

Sylvie appeared at the doorway of the kitchen. "I think it's safe to say you've made a good impression on everyone so far. Now, get your arses in my kitchen. There's work to be done!"

I gave Sylvie a salute, and she gave me the middle finger. "Isn't my mother-in-law just charming?" I laughed.

Aiden grinned and followed me into the kitchen.

The hours whizzed past, and I watched with wonder as Aiden entertained twenty four and five-year-olds. He played games, gave piggybacks, chatted with the parents who stayed to watch the madness. He was the model of parenting and kids' party perfection. I couldn't keep my eyes off him, and every time he looked in my direction, he smiled and gave the occasional cheeky wink. My heart flipped in my chest when he did, and I knew I was already done for.

"I see that look." Sylvie appeared beside me, looking at the scene in front of us.

"What look?" I tried to bluff.

She smirked. "You are screwed, my boy. Even this old fool can see that."

"Maybe." I smiled back.

"Maybe my arse." She laughed and headed back into the kitchen to clear up the dishes.

Soon, all the kids were gone, and most of the mess was cleared up. Sylvie smiled at Aiden and me. "Why don't you two bugger off? I'll finish off here, and Addison's already asleep upstairs."

"Are you sure?" I asked her.

She threw a tea towel over her shoulder. "Go for it! Get out while the night is still young and you have the chance."

I kissed her cheek. "I love you, you know that?"

"Oh, fuck off." She laughed.

Aiden snorted. "It was lovely to meet you, Sylvie." He leaned in and kissed her on the cheek.

"You too, love. Now, get out of here and take him with you before I change my mind." She grinned.

Aiden moved past me, grabbed my hand on the way, and pulled me along with him. "Let's do as she says." He raised an eyebrow as he spoke, and I smirked.

Chapter Nineteen
Aiden

I NEEDED to get out while Sylvie was willing. I had been having a blast all day long with the kids and the parents, but with the glances Ellis had been casting my way, I needed to be alone with him.

"Where are we going?" he asked when we had settled into my car and were pulling out of his street.

"I thought we could go to my place," I replied, half asking, half telling.

He smirked at me sexily. "That sounds good to me."

God, I needed to get this man back to my house as fast as I could. I needed to get him alone. I needed to see where it would lead without him running away like he did last time.

"You know, I've never asked. Where do you live?" Ellis was watching London pass by outside the car windows.

"In a nice terrace house by the Thames."

Ellis glanced over at me with suspicion. "You live in a terrace house?"

I smirked. I did, but not the kind of terrace house he probably had in his mind. "Yes, just down the street from the riverside. It's a nice neighbourhood. You can tell me what you think of it when we get there."

Ellis's brow creased as we drove along the Thames through Battersea. I knew he was trying to figure out where we were going. I turned onto Battersea Bridge Road and headed over the Thames.

"Chelsea?" he guessed.

I just laughed. "You'll see soon enough." I pulled down the narrow part of the street outside my house. I turned towards the large wooden gates and pressed the button on the fob to open them. Ellis glanced over at me. I knew this wasn't the kind of terrace he was thinking about, but from the outside, it looked like my house was a tiny bungalow shoehorned in between two rows of terrace houses. Instead, it was so much more. I pulled into my parking spot outside and smiled at Ellis. "Welcome to Casa Aiden." I pressed the start/stop button to silence the engine and got out of the car.

Ellis blinked and took in what I was doing. He got out and followed me to the front door. "Are you ready?" I smirked. He gave me a cheeky glare. I put the key in the door and in we went. As soon as we walked into my house, the room opened out into a huge living space.

Ellis gasped. "Jesus, Aiden. This place is enormous."

"Deceptive, isn't it?" I chuckled. "It's got five bedrooms, all with their own bathroom. There's an office and roof terrace above that, and there's a gym and family room down-stairs," I explained. "Come on. I'll show you."

I led Ellis around my house. I was nervous as hell. I'd never had anyone there. It was my tranquil island in a sea of chaos. No one knew where it was aside from my family. I didn't entertain there, and I certainly didn't take men there. Ellis was a first. He silently walked around my house, taking in everything, admiring all the light, airy rooms and all the space. It's funny; it had never felt empty until I showed it to him.

"You have so many rooms," Ellis mused.

I shrugged. "I have. To be honest, it's not something I had thought about until now."

He blushed. "Sorry. I didn't mean to make you feel bad about your house. It is stunningly beautiful and very deceptive from the street. I'm just blown away by how gorgeous it is."

"It's fine, honestly." I smiled. "And this is," I flicked on the light, "my bedroom."

Ellis looked at the bed, walked over, and bounced down on one side of it. "So, have you had many guys back to your house?"

Warmth washed over me. Was Ellis jealous? I walked over to him, keeping my eyes locked with his as I did. "None."

His eyes widened and his mouth fell open. "What, not ever?"

I shook my head. "Nope. Not a single one."

"Oh," he said as he looked up at me from the bed.

"I've never let anyone in this house before tonight."

He swung his legs back over the side of the bed, stood, and came back over to me. His hand skimmed over my jawline and his lips found mine. I felt what he was saying in his kiss. He was thanking me for being allowed in. There had never been any doubt in my mind that I would let him in, and to more than my house. I returned his kiss with fervour, licking along his lips, teasing his mouth open so I could let my tongue dance with his.

Ellis moaned against my mouth, and I moved us around the tiniest bit so I could press him against the wall. My hands went to his waist, and I grabbed at his clothes to pull him tight against me as our passionate kiss continued. I wanted him to know just how much I needed him in that moment. His arms snaked around my neck, holding me against his mouth.

Kissing Ellis felt like the most perfect thing I had ever experienced. The way his body moulded against mine. The way his tongue played over mine. The way he moaned softly when he felt how hard my cock was against the front of his hip. Everything about him was just perfection.

He let one of his hands drop from the back of my neck, skimming it over my whole body, touching my chest, slipping across my stomach, and heading straight down until it rested over my cock. When he rubbed along my hard length through my jeans, I gasped and broke our kiss.

We both looked down to where his hand was touching me. Ellis looked up at me with a grin, his hazel eyes shimmering with lust. I put my hands up on the wall on either side of him, just above his shoulders. I widened my stance just a fraction and waited to see what he would do next. He looked down at his hand and pressed it firmly against my throbbing cock again. I didn't know if he was teasing me or challenging me. Part of me wished he would drop to his knees, take out my dick, and slide it into his waiting, wet mouth. Another part of me wanted him to turn around, press his arse against my cock, and beg me for it inside him.

Ellis did neither.

With one hand, he undid the buttons on my shirt. The other, he kept rubbing me with, teasing me, making me want more. But he was so much of a damn turn-on that I was starting to feel more frustrated than teased, but unlike the usual frustration, this was the most delicious kind I'd ever experienced.

"Oh, fuck, Ellis." I moaned when he slid his hand over

my chest, tickling against the hairs there. His touch was exquisite, and I hungered for more. His fingers moved over my nipples, and my cock lurched in his hand. Ellis grinned and dipped his head to plant a line of kisses and licks across my chest before finally resting on my nipple, latching his mouth around it and sucking it gently.

Holy fuck. Between the pressure from his mouth and the pressure from his hand, he was going to make me so damn turned on that I would embarrass myself like a teenage schoolboy. I couldn't take it any longer, and I took a step back, my body on fire and already missing his touch. I took Ellis by the hand and led him back towards my bed, pulling my shirt from my body as I did.

I needed more of him, and I needed it now.

Chapter Twenty
Ellis

WHEN AIDEN STEPPED BACK from me, I thought for a split second that I had done something he didn't like, but when I saw the expression all over his handsome face and the fact that his dark eyes were now almost black pools of pure lust, I quickly cast those thoughts aside.

He took my hand in his and pulled me towards the bed, and I felt the electricity travel up my arm from where his skin made contact with mine. It was contact that he broke temporarily to remove his shirt. I let my eyes feast on how amazing he looked undressed, roaming all over every inch of exposed skin. I grabbed my t-shirt, pulled it off over my head, and tossed it aside. When he turned to look at me to make sure I was still coming with him towards the bed, he paused, drinking in every inch of me in return. I wasn't as athletic or as toned as Aiden, but running about after a young child kept me trim.

Aiden sat down on the side of the bed and pulled me towards him. He ran his hands up the backs of my legs before grabbing handfuls of my arse, his face nuzzling against my stomach. "Fuck, the sight of you half naked is beautiful. *You're* beautiful," he murmured against my skin.

I wasn't sure anyone had ever called me beautiful before. Handsome, sure, but beautiful was new, and it stirred up a feeling in me I had never experienced before.

He looked up at me and raised an eyebrow. His hands slid around my waist and rested on the button fly of my jeans. My breathing hitched with every pop of the buttons. Aiden's gaze never left mine. He slid my jeans down my thighs a little and then looked down to see me encased in the cotton of my boxers. My excitement for the moment was obvious. My cock tented my underwear, straining to be released. Aiden cupped my balls and my cock bobbed in reply. I hoped he wasn't going to be as torturous to me as I was to him. Fortunately, he was far too interested in what he was doing to draw it out agonisingly. His hand slid over my length, to the waistband of my boxers and tugged them down, freeing my dick, letting it bob right in front of his face.

Aiden's hand surrounded my cock, and he pumped it up and down. The feeling was so unbelievably hot. A soft moan fell from my lips. I needed more. I *wanted* more. A small smirk graced his face, and he dipped his head and slid his tongue around the head of my cock, circling it before taking more of me into his mouth.

"Oh, Jesus, Aiden," I hissed as he sucked forcefully on my rock-hard dick. It throbbed at the sensation. It had been starved of attention for what felt like forever, and it wouldn't be long before Aiden drove me over the edge. I ran my fingers through his hair and pushed him farther down against me, making him take more of my cock, sliding deeper, finding myself pushing against the resistance at the back of his throat.

He hummed in satisfaction and grabbed my arse, the vibrations adding to the sensations and driving me close to the edge. "Fuck, Aiden. You're going to make me come."

He looked up and raised his eyebrow in a challenge. He was encouraging me to do exactly that. I looked down at him and he kept looking up at me. My breathing got faster, I felt that tell-tale tightening in my nut sack, and before I could do anything else, I held Aiden's mouth secure against me and exploded down his throat.

The corners of Aiden's mouth pulled upwards, and I knew he was satisfied with the outcome. He took his time to let me finish, swallowing everything I had to give him, and licking his lips as my cock slid from between them.

"Jesus." I regretted that it hadn't taken much effort but was delighted Aiden was happy to do it. His expression broke out into a full shit-eating grin, or should that be a cum-eating grin? "You look very pleased with yourself." I smirked.

"I am, and you tasted even better than I imagined you would."

Heat crept across my face. "Damn, it's been a while since anyone said anything like that to me."

His smile faded a little. "You should be told that often."

I stroked his cheek and he stood, wrapped his arms around me, and kissed me softly. "You're a beautiful man, you taste amazing, and I want to remind you of that as much as I can." Our soft kiss grew into a fierce one, passion taking over again, and I was very much aware that even though I had been so well taken care of, Aiden hadn't. I felt his hardness pressed against me, and I knew just what I wanted him to do with it next.

I pulled back from Aiden and removed my jeans and underwear properly. I stood before him, totally naked, and started to undo the front of his jeans, needing him naked too. I clearly wasn't doing it fast enough. He yanked everything to the floor, stepped out of it, and kicked it all aside. *Holy shit*. The man looked absolutely spectacular naked. I needed my hands on him as soon as I took in all of him. I stepped back towards him and kissed him again hard, grabbing his arse and pressing myself against him to get as much skin-on-skin contact as humanly possible.

Aiden moved behind me, kissing across my chest, shoulders, and back. His hands roamed over my chest, his lips found my neck, and he pressed himself against my back. I felt his hard cock pressed between my arse cheeks, and I let out a moan.

His hands and mouth covered my skin hungrily, and I leaned back against him. "I need to be inside you," he whispered against my ear as he nuzzled against my neck. I reached behind me and slid my hands over his buttocks, pulling him harder against my arse.

"I need to feel you."

Aiden moved away from behind me, and I sighed at the loss of him. He climbed onto his bed and beckoned for me to join him. There wasn't a need to ask again.

His lips found mine again, and he pressed his body to mine. Aiden moved between my legs and started to grind against me. Large, strong hands roamed over me. His cock pulsed against my hip. Aiden's tongue plundered my mouth eagerly. He kissed down over my neck and chest, and I lifted my hips to meet his. I needed to feel him inside me. I wanted more, but I just couldn't bring myself to ask for it.

Aiden leaned over to his bedside table and produced a bottle of lube. He stared at me like a predator eyeing up its prey as he stroked the lube over his cock. He let it cover his length, and he used what was left on his fingers to spread a slick coating over my arsehole, teasing a finger inside me as he did.

"Oh, sweet fuck." I moaned, feeling him pressing against the muscle in my ass, making it give way to his fingers and feeling something inside me for the first time in what felt like a very long time.

"Your arse is so fucking hot." Aiden moaned breathlessly. My muscles clenched around him when he said it. "Ohhh, FUCK, yes!" He pulled his fingers from my ass and licked them. His wet fingers then gripped his cock and pointed it against my arse. I spread my legs wider, bringing my knees towards my chest, and Aiden pressed the head of his dick against me and pushed.

I moaned like a whore when I felt that burn as he stretched me out and entered me. It had definitely been too long since I had been fucked.

"God, Ellis, you feel so damn hot," he said, sliding deeper inside me slowly, letting me get used to his thick, long cock. I lifted my hips against him. I wanted to take him deeper; I needed to take more of him. Aiden took the hint, pulled back, and then slammed into me hard and deep with a grunt. I moaned loudly, a slight pain at the pressure of him inside me with such force which just added to the pleasure.

He pushed my legs apart and away from my chest, leaned over my body, and kissed me hard. He eased himself down over me, thrusting inside me as he did. Jesus, he was making love to me instead of just fucking me. I moaned against his mouth. He broke our kiss and looked at me as he kept up his slow and sensual pace. "Christ, you feel so good."

I closed my eyes, the feeling of him looking at me while he said sweet things and filled me so completely was too much. I was overwhelmed by how good this felt, how good he looked, and how much this was pulling in my chest. I was falling for him. Hard.

"Look at me, Ellis," he breathed.

I squeezed my eyes tighter. "I can't."

"Look. At. Me." He punctuated each word with a roll of his hips.

Oh, God. I dared a glimpse.

"Stay with me. Please." There was something in how he said *please* that undid me. I couldn't not look at him with such a plea. We locked our gaze, and I stroked my hands over his skin as he started to thrust faster into my arse. He was getting close; I could feel his cock pulsing inside me, and I kept looking deep into his eyes as I wrapped my legs around his back and surrendered to it all. I surrendered to the wash of emotion and sensation that was threatening to drown me. I surrendered to the need to have him come deep inside me. I surrendered to the feelings that had been growing for Aiden since I first met him. With my surrender came a moan from deep within him as he drove himself deep one final time, coming undone as he did and unloading deep up my arse.

His breathing was rapid, and he peppered kisses over my chest, neck, and lips before burying his head into my neck and leaning his weight against me. I wrapped my arms around him and held him against me. I didn't want him to move. I didn't want to feel the loss of him from inside me. We lay there, tangled together in silence, both of us taking in the magnitude of how we were feeling about what just happened.

Just as both of us were in danger of drifting off to sleep, Aiden moved out of me and flopped down beside me. He reached over to his other bedside table and pressed some switches. The lights dimmed, the room felt warmer, and he settled himself in against me. His arm was draped across my body, and a soft kiss was placed on my shoulder. I put my hand over his and drank in just how comfortable and easy it was to be in his presence, and I let sleep take over.

Chapter Twenty-One
Aiden

Two weeks later

WE FINALLY DID IT. The JLC deal was completed, and to celebrate, I took Ellis out to dinner. Things were moving along nicely between us too. I spent time at his house, and he spent time at mine. Every time I was with him, the surer I was that this was the man I wanted to end up with forever.

Dinner was my choice this time. I wanted it to be somewhere fancy and show him off a little, even though something inside told me that might be a very silly idea. I wined him and dined him and planned to take him back to my place again. It had been lovely, and I couldn't wait to see where else the evening would lead.

We were just leaving the restaurant as an old client of Munroe Holdings walked in the door.

"My, my, my! Little Aiden Munroe!" he exclaimed. "How the hell are you, boy?"

I shook his hand energetically and smiled. "I'm good thanks, Mr Laverty. How are your wife and daughter?"

He laughed. "The wife is still a pain in my ass. I don't

think I'll be retiring any time yet. And the daughter, well, she's made me a grandpa. How's your mum and dad?"

I laughed. "You know Mum, keeping Dad on his toes now he has all this time on his hands."

"I heard you're the big shot boss now. Good on you, lad." He patted my shoulder, and I smiled politely. He kept looking from me to Ellis and back again, and I knew he was waiting for an introduction. "Mr Laverty, this is my..." I tried to think about what I should call Ellis. I wanted to say, 'this is my boyfriend', but the words stuck in my throat. I didn't know what to call him. We hadn't really discussed what sort of label to put on things. I struggled to find the right word for him, one that my father would be able to stand behind too, and my mouth blurted something out before I had time to think it through, "...friend," I introduced. "Ellis Baxter. Ellis, meet Dave Laverty, an old client of Munroe Holdings."

Ellis smiled insincerely, his mouth distorted slightly with the sourness of the word 'friend'. I regretted my choice of word instantly. I had just panicked and didn't know what else to say. I thought about my dad and felt the need to play it down. The second the word was out of my mouth, I knew I was a coward and an idiot, but it was too late, and judging by the look on Ellis's face, the damage had been done.

Dave Laverty clearly sensed the tension that was building and moved away from us. "Tell your Dad I was asking after him." He smiled and shook my hand and Ellis's and walked away.

In complete silence, Ellis walked out of the restaurant in front of me. Not a single word was spoken until we got to my car.

"Do you want to come back to mine?" I asked, having a pretty good idea of what the answer was going to be.

"Take me home." He wouldn't even look at me. I couldn't bear it.

The farther we got out of London and towards Sutton, the more pissed off I got. I knew I shouldn't have. I knew I was completely in the wrong, but I started to feel more and more like I was between and rock and a hard place, and when in that situation, I did the only thing I could do. I reverted to being a complete prick about it.

Chapter Twenty-Two
Ellis

MY HEAD WAS SPINNING. Did I mean that little to him? Was I really going to be forever cast aside in public as a 'friend'? I didn't understand him. He was always surprising me, but this... well, this was a surprise he could shove up his arse sideways. This was not how I wanted to be treated.

I said nothing as he drove me home. I said nothing as I walked into my house and he followed, and I said nothing as I made a coffee.

"Are you going to spit it out or not?" he sneered.

"Just your 'friend', am I?" I snapped back.

"Really? What would you have me tell him, Ellis? Did you want me to tell him, 'Hi, this is the guy I like to stick my dick in. Yes, I'm a raging homo'?"

I couldn't believe he was talking to me like that. I couldn't believe he didn't think I was someone worth having more respect for. I felt like his dirty little secret. Suddenly, everything we had was seedy and dirty and cheap. I was disgusted with him and with myself for falling for someone who would ever treat me like that.

"In those words? No, not exactly what I was expecting,

but how about something as simple as 'he's my boyfriend'? Or is having a boyfriend beneath you?"

He ran his fingers through his hair. "Jesus Christ, Ellis. That's not what this is. I'm not ashamed of you, I'm just a fucking private person, okay? I have a high-profile company. I'm a high-profile person. You know this."

Really? That's a good reason for this in his book? "So fucking what, Aiden? I don't see the problem with people knowing you're gay. Jesus, that's why you were always seen with women, isn't it? You're in the fucking closet. Does your family even know?"

"Ellis," he pleaded and tried to reach out for me.

"Don't fucking touch me." I pulled away from him.

"It's not like that. My family knows I'm gay. My mum, my dad, my sister, they all know, and they have no objections to me being what I am."

I scoffed. "No objections? You make it sound like some dangerous hobby that you've taken up and they've had to approve of."

"Jesus, what the fuck do you want me to say, Ellis? I'm sorry, but I really don't understand why you need to make this such a big thing!" He was pacing like he did in a business meeting when he was under pressure. *Good!* I needed him to understand what this meant to me.

"Because it is a big fucking thing to me, okay? Do you never wonder why the only parent I talk about isn't even mine? Do you never wonder why it's just me and Sylvie? I'll tell you, shall I? Baxter is Tim's name. I took it to finally cut all ties with the mother and father that thought I was a disgusting abomination and wouldn't even speak to me after I came out to them. My mother told me I was fucking dead to her, and my father beat the living shit out of me and told me he clearly wasn't my real father because he would never have a queer kid. I was sixteen years old, Aiden. So, yes, being treated like your dirty fucking secret makes me feel just like they did when I was a kid."

He looked like I had slapped him in the face. "I didn't know," he murmured.

"Yeah, well, why the fuck would you? It's not like we've been dating that long, and I have enough baggage around me already without dumping more at your door."

His hand went to my arm and then dropped back down to his side. "I'm not publicly gay. It's something my father thought would be better for the business. He didn't think people would be respectful or pleasant, and he suggested I just didn't tell people. But I've never been in a situation where I've been out publicly with someone the way I have with you. And when that old client approached me, I panicked, and I just said you were my friend."

"Yeah, well, if you're the best kind of friend I can get, then I need a better fucking class of friend." I didn't mean to sound so much like an asshole, but fear, self-loathing, and embarrassment poured out of me. "You made me feel like nothing, Aiden."

He shook his head. "No. Jesus, no, Ellis. You are not nothing to me."

"I can't deal with this right now. You need to leave."

"Ellis!"

I shook my head. "No, Aiden. I can't. Fuck you. I'm worth so much more than that shit."

He hung his head in defeat. He didn't utter another word, and he walked out the front door, got in his car, and was gone.

My legs gave up and I sank to my knees, tears streaming down my face. I couldn't bear the thought of facing him again after this. I couldn't believe he had dismissed me so completely after everything.

What if this was it? What if it was over? I stayed on the kitchen floor and let all the emotions I had kept in for everything pour out. I was hurt by my parents, hurt by Tim's loss, and now hurt by such a rejection from Aiden.

Chapter Twenty-Three
Aiden

I drove around London aimlessly. *Why? Why am I such a fucking idiot?* Ellis was everything to me, and in a moment of panic, I had ruined it all.

I wanted to stand up and tell Dave Laverty that Ellis was my boyfriend and we were on a date, but I just kept thinking of my dad's advice to me when I took over, that people were assholes, and it was probably better to keep my private life private.

I hadn't known about his family. That just made me feel sick. Why hadn't he told me? Thinking about him and his family made me think of mine. And my aimlessness turned to the direction of my family home of the last thirty-six years.

"You're like a bear with a sore head. What the actual fuck is wrong with you?" Jennie glared.

I shrugged at my sister. "Like I have any fucking clue what you're talking about."

"Oh, you don't? Did he dump you?"

"Dump *me*?" I choked. Had he dumped me? Was that what this was? "No... No, I dumped *him*, okay?"

Jennie laughed in my face. "Oh, yeah. I forgot that the mighty Aiden Munroe would never be dumped ever, would he?"

"Go fuck yourself."

"Aiden Carter Munroe, that better not be how you speak to your sister," my mum scolded.

"Sorry, Mother."

"Ha! Dumped and now scolded. This day keeps getting better and better."

"Jennifer."

I wasn't the only one being scolded. I grinned at my sister and stuck my tongue out behind my mum's back.

"I saw that, Aiden."

"Sorry, Mother."

Jennie came over beside me. "So, what the hell happened?" she whispered.

I shook my head.

"It was the dad stuff, wasn't it?"

Mum looked over at us. "What 'Dad stuff', Jennie?"

I sighed, and Jennie started to explain it. "The stuff with Dad and his opinion that Aiden shouldn't be out with men in public."

My mum shook her head. "Still? Son, I didn't know you were still actively listening to that." Mum was surprised. So was I. I didn't think she would have wanted me to go against what my dad was saying when it came to the business. "Your father is old-fashioned. He thinks people are too, but he doesn't realise they have moved into the 21st Century and left him behind. You are an intelligent and successful businessman. What you decide for your company is good enough."

I shook my head.

"Son. I love your dad, and I know you worship the man, but that doesn't mean I agree with everything he has to say. When it comes to this, he's wrong. You deserve to be happy. You deserve to live your life how you want to."

She pulled me into a tight hug, and Jennie hugged the back of me too. Tears prickled my eyes. I was blessed to have a family who loved me. I thought about what Ellis had told me about his parents disowning him when he admitted he was gay. My heart broke even more. I was truly a giant cock.

"Oh, Mum. I've made a right mess of things." A tear rolled down my cheek.

"Tell us what happened," Jennie prompted.

I started at the beginning. I told them about what happened with the date and meeting up with Dave Laverty. I told them about what I had said. Jennie hissed at me.

"Really, Aiden?"

"I didn't think, okay!" I protested.

Mum took my hand in hers. "Calm down and finish the story."

I poured out everything else. I told them Ellis had told me about his family, how they had deserted him. How they had abused him just for being gay. Tears fell down all our faces, and Jennie and Mum hugged me tight again.

"What do I do, Mum?" I asked her.

She smiled and wiped my face. "Well, you're your father's son, you know. You both have an amazing knack of fucking things up."

Jennie stood opened-mouthed at the f-word falling out of our mother's mouth.

"Mother!" she scolded.

"Oh, hush. You know it's true. That's why the pair of them butt heads so damn often. You're all right, Jennie. My genes seem to have overruled the bullshit ones your dad gave you."

The serious look on my mum's face made both Jennie and I erupt into laughter. Dad, with perfect timing, picked that moment to walk into the kitchen.

"Something funny?" he asked.

Mum kissed him and hooked her arm around his. "Nothing you need to worry about. Now, Aiden needs to talk to you about something. And Carter. You listen to our son, do you understand?"

Dad rolled his eyes. "Yes, dear."

He nodded his head for me to follow and we headed towards his study.

"Now, what is it you need to talk to me about?" he said, sitting behind his desk.

"I've met someone," I blurted out.

Dad nods. "Well, it's about time."

"And I want to be open about my relationship with him."

He stared at me, and I felt like I was a naughty kid getting ready for a lecture from the headmaster, not a grown man having a conversation with his dad. "You know my thoughts on that as far as the business is concerned, son."

I sighed. "I know, Dad. But... well, do you think I understand the business we're in?"

Dad nodded.

"And do you think I'm good at it? Do you think I would do anything to hurt the company?"

Dad sighed. "Son, I wouldn't have retired as early as I did if I thought you weren't capable of running it. But some of the old goats we deal with year in and year out... they're not as okay with that kind of thing."

"Dad, the word is gay. I'm gay, and I've hidden it for a long time because of the company. But I want a life. I've met someone, and I want to be with him properly. I want to be able to introduce him at events as my boyfriend, or my partner, or even my husband if I thought he was willing to have me."

"Your son is in love, Carter." Mum stood in the doorway of Dad's study. "You remember what that's like, don't you?"

"Get in here." Dad sighed, beckoning Mum over to him. She walked past me and went to where he sat on his chair. He patted his lap, and she moved herself to hold onto his neck and sit on his knee. "You know only too well that I still know exactly what it's like to be in love, Mrs Munroe," he teased her. "But this is business."

Mum looked at him and raised an eyebrow at him. *Oh, shit. He's in trouble.* "Carter Joseph Munroe, this is the 21st bloody Century, your son is gay, and all he's asking for is for you to stop being such an old-fashioned git and leave him to run the company to the best of his ability and to live his life how he sees fit. Is that such a problem? Are you ashamed of having a gay son?"

Dad knew when he was beaten. "I will never be ashamed of Aiden being gay. I have no problems with it. I said to him just before you interrupted that it's about time he found someone."

"Well then, Aiden is the CEO of Munroe Holdings, and the last time I checked, he didn't actually need your permission to conduct business as he thinks appropriate. Am I right?"

"Yes, dear." Dad had given up.

"So, I guess tomorrow, Aiden, you're going to be able to

make whatever business decision you think will work. What do you think?" She beamed in my direction with a wink.

I grinned at her. "Thank you, Dad. I won't let you down and you won't regret this."

"Lift your arse off my lap, woman." He attempted to get up and get Mum off his knee. Mum moved, and Dad came around the desk. His arms went straight around me, and he held me in a tight hug. "Son, I have never once been let down by you. You are my flesh and blood, and I've been proud of you since the moment you were born. I just want you happy, and I feared idiots would make your life harder if they knew." While his logic was off by a mile, his intentions were flawless. He had wanted to protect me. Protect the business and the family. I hugged him back just as tight.

"Thanks, Dad. I love you."

"I love you too, son."

Chapter Twenty-Four
Aiden

When I arrived at work the next week, there was no sign of Ellis at his desk. By ten in the morning, I called Liz to find out what was going on.

"He needs some personal time. He says he doesn't know when he'll be back."

"Fuck. Have you got anyone that can cover, even for today?"

"Sorry, Mr Munroe. No one is free today. I can have someone in place for you by tomorrow if that's okay."

"Right. I guess."

"I'll send you their details later in the day."

I didn't wait to hear her say anything else before hanging up. He was hiding from me, and I knew it. Jesus, I really had fucked up big time, and needed to sort this out. There had to be a way to get him back. Maybe it was to come clean and out myself. I was also getting an idea of just how to do that.

There was a London business news show that had been trying to get an interview with me for a long time, and because of everything Dad had always said, I had refused. I was familiar enough with the show to know that it would eventually come around to questions on my personal life.

I lifted the phone, and I called the producer who gave me her card about sixteen months ago. "Erica? Aiden Munroe here. Are you still looking for that interview?" I pulled my phone from my ear when she shrieked with delight. "I'm going to assume that means yes." I laughed.

"Mr Munroe, you know I've been trying to get you on our show for well over a year now. You're about the only man in London who hasn't spoken to us yet!"

I shook my head with a smile. "I have a condition for you, Erica, and if you can't meet it, I'll be calling the next producer who has been hounding me. Understand?"

"Anything," she agreed, and I outlined to her exactly what I wanted, and when the interview needed to happen.

When I was done with the arrangements for the interview, I called a florist and arranged to have a huge bunch of flowers sent to Sylvie with a note telling her all about the interview, that I knew I had fucked up, and that I needed her to get Ellis to watch it. I didn't know if it was going to work, but it was the best shot I had of getting him back.

***

It was a long week without Ellis, but I was feeling confident that my plan would work. I stood on the edge of the set in the TV studio on Friday evening, nervous about being on television, and more nervous about whether or not Sylvie was on my side, and if Ellis would be watching.

"And next on the show, we have Aiden Munroe."

I smiled politely, walked onto the set, and settled myself at the desk opposite the presenter, Gaynor.

"Thank you so much for being here, Aiden. I know we've been trying to get you onto the show for a long time."

I nodded. "Thanks, Gaynor. It's lovely to be here. I've been incredibly busy, as you can imagine."

"Indeed. One of the youngest CEOs in London, and not without your doubters initially."

I knew what she meant. Plenty of people had just assumed that it was the fact that I was my father's son that led me to the position and not any real skill. "Well, when you take over from your father, it's going to happen, really, isn't it? But that was three and a half years ago now, and I feel that the prosperity the company is experiencing more than illustrates my ability in the position."

Gaynor smiled. "I agree. I know that just recently you have had a very successful deal for several properties with JLC?"

Someone had done their homework for the show. I nodded. "Yes. We recently acquired forty-three of their properties. I'm very happy with how that deal turned out. It has increased our portfolio, and we will soon have new tenants in those properties."

"You take care of your tenants and the properties they're in."

I nodded. "Yes. Munroe Holdings has always had a reputation of being a company based on family values. We don't treat people as a cash commodity. They are human beings, and these are their homes."

Gaynor nodded. "You value family, and your company has always had that reputation. Do you have a family, Aiden?"

Finally, we got to the questions I knew they really wanted to ask. I shook my head. "Other than my parents and sister, no. Not at the minute."

She nodded. "Is that something you would like? To get married and have a family?"

I smiled. "Well, I'm gay, so my method of getting a family might be a little unusual, but I would love to have a husband and get married and have some children with him."

I prayed Ellis was watching this. I saw the presenter's face when I said it; she looked like she'd won the television journalist's version of the lottery. In a way, I guess she had. She'd just out-scooped everyone else who had ever tried to get me for an interview.

"Has being gay provided you any difficulties in the business world?" She didn't falter; she was a complete professional at handling the bombshell I had dropped in her lap.

"To be honest, I've kept my private life very much out of the public eye. It wasn't anyone else's business, and I didn't need to have it printed up in gutter rags when they were having a slow news day."

"So, what changed?" She went straight to the point. I think she knew only too well that there was a good reason for my sudden change of mind.

I smiled and looked at her and gave a small side glance to the camera. *Please God be watching this, Ellis.* "I met someone, and for the first time in my life, I can see myself settling down and having a family, and that's something I can't hide so easily. That's something I want to be shouting from the rooftops."

Gaynor grinned. She had the scoop. I was gay. I was in love. I was ready to tell the world.

"Does this person have a name?"

I nodded. "He's called Ellis, and he's the most amazing man I've ever met."

Gaynor nodded, chatted about other stuff, and introduced other panel members. I sat the whole time hoping that Sylvie had got the flowers, read the card, and that Ellis had seen everything.

Chapter Twenty-Five
Sylvie

I was stunned when the flowers arrived at the door. I thought Rodney was still trying to kiss my ass after the miserable time I had on our last date, or at least I did until I read the card.

> *Sylvie,*
>
> *I have been a complete prick. I don't deserve Ellis. But I would like your help to make everything okay again. I'm going to tell everyone that I'm gay on the London Business Tonight show this Friday. All I ask is that you get Ellis to watch. I love your son-in-law with all my heart. He's right, I shouldn't be keeping him a secret.*
>
> *Aiden xo*

Well, that wasn't what I had expected. I understood why my boy was so pissed off at Aiden. His family had hurt him so much by rejecting him for being gay, and part of him felt like Aiden was doing the same thing. But this old girl saw it differently. I understood where Aiden was coming from too.

He loved his family, he respected his father, and he didn't want to disappoint him. Hell, I even understood where Aiden's dad was coming from. People are assholes, and sharing that you're gay, as Ellis knew too well, can be a recipe for hurt. He was, with a warped logic, protecting his son.

I didn't know what to do for the best, but I knew Ellis was hurting, and I would have done anything to put the smile back on that boy's face.

"Ellis, stick that TV on, will you? And put it on to ITV," I called from the kitchen as I made us both a cup of tea.

"London Business Tonight? Sylvie, when the fuck did you start paying attention to business news?"

I grinned at him as I walked in and set his cup of tea in front of him. "Since you started working for Mr Hotty. Have you seen some of the businessmen in London, love? I'm old, not dead. I might find someone to go and work for myself." I laughed.

"Jesus, you get worse." Ellis laughed at me and drank his tea.

I cuddled in against my son-in-law, hoping it would be enough to trap him and stop him from leaving once Aiden was on the screen.

"And next on the show, we have Aiden Munroe."

Ellis looked at me. "Did you know about this?"

I shrugged. "I don't know what you mean. Now shut up. I'm trying to listen."

I could feel his eyes boring into me as I pretended to not notice and keep watching the TV. As much as he might temporarily hate me for making him watch and tricking him, I knew how much he still felt for Aiden, and I knew he wouldn't be able to not watch.

"Is that something you would like? To get married and have a family?" the presenter asked him.

Aiden smiled widely; he was proud of what he was about to say. "Well, I'm gay, so my method of getting a family might be a little unusual, but I would love to have a husband and get married and have some children with him."

Ellis gripped my hand tightly. "Did he just…"

"Sshhhh!"

He stopped, and we both sat there in silence for the next few minutes.

"So, what changed?" he was asked.

"I met someone, and for the first time in my life, I could see myself settling down and having a family, and that's something I can't hide so easily. That's something I want to be shouting from the rooftops."

The presenter was starting to look like the cat that got the cream. "Does this person have a name?"

I held my breath; so did Ellis. "He's called Ellis, and he's the most amazing man I've ever met."

I looked at him as a tear slid from his eye and soaked his cheek. I squeezed the hand that was still in mine.

"Tell me I'm not dreaming, Sylvie," he whispered to me.

"No, son. This is real. Mr Hotty just went on TV and declared he's gay and that he's in love with you." More tears fell, and I pulled him in against me for a hug. "I told you, my boy. He loves you."

He shook his head. "I can't believe he did that… And I can't believe that you were in on it!"

"Well, how the hell else would you have seen it?" I laughed, and he glared at me.

"He can't just declare it on there and expect me to be over it and think everything's okay!"

"He won't. But he had to start somewhere, and I think as starting gestures go, that's a pretty good one."

Ellis agreed. "I think I need to go back to work."

I grinned. "I think you do, and I think my work here is done." I lifted my cup and shuffled off to the kitchen with it.

Chapter Twenty-Six
Aiden

WHEN I WALKED into the building on Monday morning, my heart was heavy. I hadn't heard anything from Ellis. I didn't know if he had seen the show, or worse, that he had seen it and just didn't care. The lift opened onto my floor, and I couldn't believe my eyes. Ellis was sitting at his desk.

I smiled broadly at him. "Morning, Ellis."

"Morning, Mr Munroe," he said, not even smiling. I sighed. He hadn't seen it. He didn't know, and he was just back at work.

"Nice to see you back." I smiled meekly.

"Liz couldn't find someone to cover and asked me to come back."

I nodded and headed into my office.

I sat down behind my desk with a sigh, all my hopes deflating as the breath left my body. I was defeated.

About an hour later, there was a knock at the door, and I looked up as Ellis entered with my coffee, muffin, and his iPad, ready to go over the day.

"Thank you," I said and lifted my coffee to go and look out the window as he spoke. I couldn't bear to look at him knowing I had messed everything up with no idea of how to get it back to where it should be.

He reviewed the day. Mostly run-of-the-mill stuff. We had a new acquisition coming up, and later there would be a meeting to discuss the options and viability of the move so soon after the JLC deal.

"Will there be anything else, Mr Munroe?"

God, I wanted to hear him calling me Aiden again. "No, Mr Baxter. That's everything. Thank you." I heard the office door closing and sighed. This time, I flopped down onto my office sofa and covered my face with a cushion, cursing everything that had led me up to this point.

***

A few hours later, I was still sitting on the sofa, wallowing in my own misery, when there was another knock at the door. Ellis walked in carrying some food and set it down on the table in front of me. "I thought you could do with some lunch."

I snorted. "I don't have much of an appetite."

"Self-pity doesn't suit you."

"Excuse me?"

"You heard me."

He said nothing else. He turned and walked back out of my office. I looked at the food he had brought in. Teriyaki steak from Wagamama and a Buddha beer. I closed my eyes and felt my heart splinter even further.

He had been right, though. The smell of the food was driving me crazy, and my stomach had started to growl in response. I needed to eat.

Just as I was thinking of giving up for the day, there was another knock at the door, and a delivery person walked in with a bunch of red roses. "Mr Munroe?" he asked. I nodded, signed for the delivery, and looked at them. Ellis was nowhere to be seen as the delivery man left. I set the flowers on my desk and lifted the card from the middle.

I saw it. I'm proud of you.
   Ellis xox

My heart flipped in my chest. He'd seen the TV show; the message to Sylvie had worked. I smiled and smelled the gorgeous roses. I was the first to admit that I probably had more work to do, but I had made a good start. Now I couldn't wait to see what the next day would bring.

Chapter Twenty-Seven
Ellis

WHEN I WALKED BACK into the office that morning, it took everything I had to keep a straight face and be as blank as possible. It wasn't so much that I wanted to torture him, even though I did, a little, it was just that I didn't want him to know I had seen the show just yet. He wasn't going to get off so easily so soon.

I got him his usual coffee and muffin and went over the day with him. I kept it strictly business. I didn't call him Aiden, and I didn't smile. It was hard. I could see his guilt, I could see that he was hurt, and all I really wanted to do was make him feel better.

The day dragged with the approach I was taking. Eventually, lunch time arrived, and Aiden hadn't left his office all day. I headed out to Wagamama and bought him back the same food we had eaten on our first lunch together. When I knocked on the door and walked in, he was still sitting on the sofa. He hadn't moved from there in hours; he had a face like thunder. I set the food down on the table in front of him. He was grumpy and snippy, and so was I, but there was nothing else I could say. I turned and walked back out of his office and closed the door.

I sat down at my desk with a sigh. Aiden Munroe was the most infuriating man I had ever met. I opened the website of a florist's that he had me use from time to time. I picked a large bouquet of red roses with a simple card and an equally simple message. I typed the message into the box.

I saw it. I'm proud of you.
   Ellis xox

I hit 'Submit' and arranged for a delivery for later that afternoon; late enough that I could escape before they arrived, but not so late that Aiden wouldn't be in his office to receive them.

By the time five p.m. arrived, Aiden was still in his office, everything was reasonably quiet, and the delivery was due in half an hour. I decided it was the perfect time to leave him to his misery. I packed up my things and headed home for the day.

The next morning, I got to work and did what I always did. I took Aiden his coffee and muffin and opened his diary on the iPad to go over the day's appointments and meetings. Today, I smiled. I still called him Mr Munroe, but things went reasonably well.

The day after, I started the day the same way again. Things relaxed, and I let them. I wanted things to get back to how they had been before the night we went to dinner. I wanted him to feel good around me again.

The next day, I called him Aiden again. I looked at his expression when I did. He stared; that predatory look had returned. I bit my lip. *Damn.*

I brought him in the lunch he had asked for. He smiled at me; a full grin. "Will there be anything else?" I smiled back.

He opened his food and breathed in the smell. "Just one thing."

I looked at him questioningly.

"Can we talk about what happened on the TV show that night?"

My eyes opened wide in surprise. "Oh. Umm."

"You saw it, right?"

He knew I did. I looked at him.

"You heard what I said."

A statement of fact, not a question. He stood up and walked over to me. He took my hand in his. "Please, Ellis." I looked at him and I couldn't take it anymore. I felt like I had tortured him enough, and when he touched me, I couldn't resist. I pressed my lips against his and pulled him against me.

Chapter Twenty-Eight
Aiden

I HAD HAD ENOUGH of the playing around. Of the avoidance of the public declaration I had made. "Please, Ellis." I reached for his hand. Every inch of my skin prickled with electrical energy when I touched him again. The next thing I knew, his mouth was on mine. I felt like a man who had been dying of thirst, only to finally be granted a drink of water. I kissed him back with a hunger I had never felt before in my life. I had missed him, and now I had him back, I never wanted the feeling to stop, and I would have done anything to keep him this time.

He took a step back, breathless. "What made you change your mind?"

"You did."

He raised an eyebrow.

"Losing you, thinking I might never see you again, never mind get to kiss you or hold you again."

Ellis blushed. The pink flush on his cheeks suited him. "Is that it?" He smirked.

"No. It might also have had something to do with the fact that, even though I'm the most cynical bastard I know, it can be as simple as looking down and seeing your hand entwined with mine and feeling like it's fucking home. Because you are my last thought every night before I sleep and my first thought every morning when I wake up. Because even if this doesn't last, and I pray to God it does, I will be forever changed for just having you in my life, no matter how long that is. Because you make me want to be a better man, more confident, surer of my place in the world. The best, most fulfilled version of me that I can be. And if that's not enough to have you back in my life, that doesn't change the fact that I am now, and always will be yours. Even if forty years from now I am happily married to someone else, I'm still yours right down in my very soul."

A tear slid down my cheek. Ellis's thumb swept across my skin as he cupped my face, his lips crushed against mine, and the softest, most tender kiss I'd ever had in my life was offered to me.

"I love you," I whispered against his lips when he paused and rested his forehead against mine.

"You hurt me."

I winced. It wasn't enough. I had been an utter wanker and lost the only thing that would ever truly make me happy for the rest of my life.

"You have to promise me you'll never do that again."

Was he forgiving me? "I promise." I was shocked, and he soothed me by pressing his lips against mine again, only this time, with more passion. His hands ran down my back and pulled me hard against him.

"I love you too," he told me.

"Say that again?"

"I said, I love you too!" He laughed.

"That's the most perfect thing I've heard my whole life." I grinned. "I know I've let you down immensely. You deserve better. So much better, and I want to spend the rest of my life making it up to you if you'll let me."

Ellis grinned. "I'll check my diary."

He leaned in and kissed me again, and I knew I could never let this man out of my life ever again. I would spend forever making sure he knew just how amazing I thought he was.

Epilogue
Ellis

Four years later

AIDEN WAS true to his word. He's been making it up to me a hell of a lot over the last few years. He made it up to me a hell of a lot two years ago, when we got married. Addison made the prettiest little bridesmaid in the world, and it was that day that she asked him if it was okay if she called him 'Daddy Aiden'. He looked like he was so proud he was going to burst, and I was too. We were becoming a family, and it was a family that included the four of us. Sylvie gave me away, and we all moved into Aiden's massive house in Chelsea.

Aiden grabbed my hand as we looked at the screen. "Everything is looking very good," the doctor told us. "Oh..."

Aiden's grip on my hand tightened. "What? Oh, God. What's wrong?"

The doctor laughed. "Mr Munroe, there's nothing to

worry about. Nothing's wrong. It's just that..." He pointed to something on the screen. "...see that?"

We both screwed up our faces and peered at the screen, trying to make out what he was pointing at.

"That would be baby number two."

My heart stopped.

"Twins?" Emma, our surrogate, grinned.

The doctor nodded. "Two babies. Everything is looking good, and they are far enough apart in there that I would guess that they are going to be non-identical. Looked like two out of the four embryos have implanted."

Tears were streaming down my husband's face when I looked at him. "One from each of us."

I shook my head with a smile. "You don't know that."

The doctor chuckled. "It's possible. You might just as easily have two from one of you. We did insert four."

Aiden shook his head. "No. I know it's one from each of us."

I laughed at his optimism. We had four donor eggs. Two of them were fertilised with Aiden's sperm, and two of them were fertilised with mine. He looked at me intently, and he reached for Emma's hand. "Thank you." He grinned. "And thank you," he said, looking at me, and kissing me softly.

The enormity of the situation hit me. "We're going to have two babies. Double the sleepless nights. Double the dirty nappies." *Oh, shit.*

Nothing was going to dull Aiden's enthusiasm. "I know! Isn't it fantastic!" Emma and the doctor laughed at him, and I groaned.

When we arrived home, Addison came running to the door. "Did you see the baby?"

Aiden picked her up and threw her over his shoulder. "Where's Nanna?" He laughed.

She appeared around the corner from the kitchen. "Well?" she asked, expectation on her face.

"Sit. We have a picture to show you." I smiled.

Sylvie and Addison sat on the sofa and looked at us. Aiden gave me a sideward glance with a grin.

"I don't want you to overreact," Aiden told them both.

"Is there something wrong?" Sylvie asked.

I shook my head. "Nothing like that."

Addison looked at us. Sylvie looked at us.

"Oh, for fuck's sake, spit it out!" she exclaimed.

Aiden smirked. "Language, Nan!" he scolded and handed her the image from the ultrasound scan. "It's twins. There are two babies!" He beamed.

Addison started jumping up and down.

Sylvie was actually speechless; something I'm not sure I'd ever seen before.

"Are you happy for us?" Aiden asked her.

Tears slid down her face and she nodded. She stood and pulled Aiden and me tight against her. "I've never been so proud of my boys."

Tears fell from my face and Aiden's as Sylvie and Addison hugged us tight. Our family was about to grow, and I couldn't wait to see what the future held for us. I would never have imagined when I walked into Aiden's office that morning that it would end up like this, but I wouldn't have had it any other way. This was how things were meant to be, and I looked forward to my forever with Aiden and our family.

---

*If you liked this, join the newsletter and find out about more
books from Drew!
www.drewduncanbooks.co.uk/newsetter*

Other Books by Drew Duncan

Just Because Series

Because I Need You

Because I Want Him

Because I Didn't Know

Because It's Always You (Coming Soon)

Standalones

Hart Beats

EROTIC SHORTS

His Rules Series

Playing by the Rules

Changing the Rules

About the Author

Drew is an Irish author with a panache for sarcasm and a love of the random, her cynicism knows no bounds, but she's a secret hopeless romantic who likes to let her characters sizzle on the pages.

She lives her with two children, and dreams of escaping to Hampshire, the home of Jane Austen. When she's not writing, you can find her knitting, crocheting, shouting at Ireland playing rugby, and of course reading.

Keep up to date with all the latest releases and info from Drew by joining their mailing list here:
www.drewduncanbooks.co.uk/newsetter

www.ingramcontent.com/pod-product-compliance
Lightning Source LLC
Chambersburg PA
CBHW030836200726
48285CB00007B/2462